Charles Mackay, Eric Mackay

Gossamer and Snowdrift

The posthumous Poems

Charles Mackay, Eric Mackay

Gossamer and Snowdrift
The posthumous Poems

ISBN/EAN: 9783337158170

Printed in Europe, USA, Canada, Australia, Japan

Cover: Foto ©Andreas Hilbeck / pixelio.de

More available books at **www.hansebooks.com**

GOSSAMER AND SNOWDRIFT

THE POSTHUMOUS POEMS

OF

CHARLES MACKAY,

LL.D., F.S.A.

AUTHOR OF "THE SALAMANDRINE," "EGERIA," "STUDIES FROM THE ANTIQUE,"
"INTERLUDES AND UNDERTONES," ETC.

WITH AN INTRODUCTION

BY HIS SON

ERIC MACKAY,

Author of "Love Letters of a Violinist."

GEORGE ALLEN

8, BELL YARD, TEMPLE BAR, LONDON

AND

SUNNYSIDE, ORPINGTON

1890

INTRODUCTION.

THE name of Charles Mackay is so well known in England and America, and his fame as a poet is so firmly established, that it is scarcely necessary for me to go into the matter at any length. His poetry has the vital glow; his songs are marked for immortality. They have the glamour of truth about them. And what says Emerson? "He who writes to his own heart writes to an eternal public." Such was eminently the case with Charles Mackay,—the People's Poet, as he is fondly called by hundreds of thousands, —one who loved Nature and human nature, and wrote of both in clear, outspoken tones,—a lark singing in the dawn of a new day, and having at heart the welfare of humanity. His was a life of labour and much happiness, for he loved work; and though he suffered in many ways,—as who has not?—he kept his mind erect (if I may so express it) even when, in the end, his body was bent down by age and care; and he waited without alarm the approach of death, which, taking him as it did on the eve of Christmas Day 1889, left in his place a bright and honoured memory, dear to England, which, sooner or later, will do him ampler justice, and dear to Scotland, his native country, which inspired some of his noblest verse.

There are other poets now living amongst us; but where is Charles Mackay's successor? He was the last of the great song-writers! Armies have marched to the words of "Cheer, boys, cheer!" and nations, dating from 1848, have found their watchword and their rallying-cry in the "Good Time Coming." The Fifth Continent —as Australia is sometimes called—was peopled, so to speak, at his voice, and empires yet to be will remember the songs which, forty years ago, he wrote for emigrants, songs which for fire and pathos, and clear and ringing patriotism, have few equals in our tongue.

It is not for me, as Charles Mackay's son, to criticise his numerous works in prose and verse,—

for some have entered the language as classics; but I may be allowed to say that, in the opinion of competent judges, his name will live as that of a true and earnest Singer. He is the Burns of the Nineteenth Century, the Béranger of English literature. And these, his last poems, the proof-sheets of which he did not live to correct, though he arranged their different headings as they are here produced, will assuredly command attention. The lyrics entitled " Life, Death and Immortality " are pregnant with great thoughts, and prove in unmistakable terms how deep was the faith he held,—how little he feared the Death which set him free,—how grand was the future beyond the tomb to which he looked forward with a fixed and radiant gaze, clouded at times by tears, but never by doubt, and always from first to last a seer as well as a poet, who, in his own words, " put on his singing-robes cheerily in the face of heaven and nature " and wore them manfully to the end.

ERIC MACKAY.

October 15th. 1890.

CONTENTS.

PART I.

BALLADS AND LYRICS.

PART II.

THISTLEDOWN AND HIGHLAND HEATHER.

PART III.

LIFE, DEATH, AND IMMORTALITY.

APPENDIX.

CHARLES MACKAY'S LAST POEM.

PART I.

BALLADS AND LYRICS.

AT RANDOM SOWN.

I scattered my rhymes on the barren ground,
   Nought was its barrenness to me ;
Or cast them adrift on the vagrant winds,
   And the stormy billows of the sea.
I never cared, or sought to know,
   Whether like fruitful seeds they grew,
Whether they perished as soon as born,
   Or faded away like the morning dew ;
Whether men heeded them or despised ;—
   For the light must shine, the lark must sing,
And the rose unfold its blushing buds
   To the warm embraces of the spring.

And yet, though careless as the flowers
   That shed their odours on the air,
I dreamed a dream that grew to a hope,
   That as the thistledown might bear
A living germ in its small balloon,
   Some of my fancies, robed in rhyme,

Might fall perchance upon fruitful soil,
 And root and ripen in their time,—
Ripen in hearts as yet unborn,
 To strengthen the weak, console the poor,
To cheer the brave in their conquering march,
 And teach the wretched to endure.
Life's hard battle permits no truce,
 And every age needs warriors strong;
And even a Rhyme may pierce like a sword
 The armour that protects the wrong!

THE GREAT WORLD AND THE POET.

"At God's great table is there room for me?"
Enquired the Poet, in his youthful glee:
"I'm strong of purpose, and content to toil,
But cannot spin, or weave, or delve the soil;
I have no knowledge of the 'bought' or 'sold,'
And cannot barter honesty for gold!
I can do nothing,—but, like bird on spray,
Or lark that soars to hail the dawning day,
Or tender nightingale that all night long
Pours to the listening world its rapturous song,
'Tis mine to sing, with earnest voice and clear,
My songs of hope and joy for men to hear,
Until their hearts throb, and their eyes illume;—
At God's great table, tell me is there room?"
  The Great World answered, "All the seats are
      taken—
Not one is void, or like to be forsaken;
The fighters, and the doers, and the traders,
Fill them all up, and suffer no invaders;

But thou canst take thy choice, and watch, and wait
For falling crumbs that haply, soon or late,
May be thy dole in the distressful hour
When strength should fail and sorrows overpower;
Why shouldst thou murmur?   If it give thee
    pleasure
To ease thy heart in thy melodious measure,
And charm the nations, thou art overpaid
In the enjoyment thou thyself hast made,—
I need thee not, and cannot give thee gold.
Poets were many in the days of old,
And these suffice me.   Great is thy reward
If far Futurity shall hail thee 'Bard!'
And carve thy name on the recording stone,
To make thy virtues and thy merits known.
So shall admiring crowds, as yet unborn,
Wipe out remembrance of the bygone scorn,
And yield their useless homage at thy tomb:"
Sing on, O Poet,—and accept thy doom!

EPICURUS AND THE SPHINX.

I.

Oh, melancholy Sphinx! the haunting glare
     Of thy stone eyes
Vexes my soul, and goads me to despair
     With mysteries
Too deeply hidden in the vast unknown
For narrow Reason, on her doubtful throne,
     To probe and scan.
Why ask me to declare what Nature is,
And why God fashioned for their bale or bliss
     The Earth and Man?

II.

And why the Evil which we feel and see
     In Nature's scheme
Should be a fact in cruel Destiny,
     And not a dream?
And why it should, since Time's perplexing birth,
Over our lovely and prolific Earth
     Its shadow cast,

And track the populous planets on their way,
Lord of the Present and the Future day,
    As of the Past?

III.

Why should I strive to see the reason why,
    Through narrow chinks?
Dark are thy riddles, and beyond reply,
    Oh, torturing Sphinx!
If Good for ever is at war with Ill,
And Good is God's unconquerable will,
    I'll seek no more
To solve the mystery of His design,
Beyond the scope of reason to define,
    On Time's dark shore.

IV.

I am—I think—I love; and while I live
    And it is Day,
I will enjoy the blessings it can give
    While yet I may.
Joy breathes around me in the wholesome air;
All Nature smiles: the Universe is fair
    With heavenly light;—
For me, the sun downpours its rays of gold,
The rivers roll, and all the flowers unfold
    Their blossoms bright.

v.

For me the stars the eloquent sky illume;
      For me the Spring
Inspires with love and joy and fruitful bloom
      Each living thing;
For me the grapes grow mellow on the stalk;
For me wit sparkles and old sages talk
      Of noble deeds;
The blythe lark carols in the light of morn;
The reapers mow the golden-bearded corn
      To serve my needs.

vi.

For me the vintage sparkles in the bowl,
      And woman's wiles,
Sweet as herself, invade my heart and soul,
      That love her smiles.
Oh, Sphinx! thy riddles shut the daylight out,
Faith is the anchor of the true devout,
      And Hope their guide;
And when my last hour comes, may every friend
Say I lived bravely till the destined end—
      And bravely died!

MY MUSES.

I CANNOT think apart
  From the mountain and the sea,
From the dew upon the grass,
  From the daisy on the lea,
From the forest leaves that whisper
  Where the wild wind passes by,
From the clouds that float like ships
  On the ocean of the sky,
From the stars that gem the darkness
  Of the deep eternal blue,
From the foam-crests of the billows
  And the dip of the sea-mew,
From the prattle of the children,
  From the look that understands,
From the smile of true affection,
  From the grasp of friendly hands,
From the peal of happy laughter,
  From the sympathy of tears,

From the solitude that teaches,
  From society that cheers.

All nature is my comrade,
  My teacher and my friend;
My best of boon companions,
  To give, to share, to lend:
It feeds my heart and spirit
  Whenever I would write,
And guides me and inspires me
  In all that I indite.

Idle the song or poem
  May seem to sordid men;
But Heart is in my meaning,
  And Love is in my pen!

ODOURS.

CRUSH me, proud world! as Beauty crushes
  The floweret that adorns her breast,
And breathes the balmy scent that gushes
  From the fair petals she has press'd;
Yes! crush me, if 'tis Fate's decree;
  Perchance the odours that exhale
At Sorrow's heavy hand may be
  Refreshing to the wayward gale;
And footsore travellers passing by
  May breathe and bless me in a sigh!

THE SECRET DRAWER.

In idle mood I touched the springs
  That opened wide the secret drawer,
To gaze on half forgotten things
  That waked the memories of yore,—
Small scraps of letters loosely tied
  With silken bands of faded blue,
Containing words of love and pride
  Wrung from my heart when life was new;

A lock of radiant golden hair
  That once adorned a glorious head
Of a young angel, heavenly fair,
  And long since numbered with the dead;
A dark brown tress—the sole remains
  Of a brave woman lost and gone,
The partner of my joys and pains,
  Whose smile made sunlight where it shone.

I sighed, I kissed them like a fool—
  Although perhaps the fool was wise

With wisdom learned in sorrow's school—
  Who saw the truth through all disguise.
And taking counsel with my thought,
  I asked myself, 'mid haze of tears,
Why these fond relics, fancy-fraught,
  Should live beyond my span of years?—

Live with their tale of thought or deed,
  For merchandise in scandal's mart,
To satisfy the clamorous greed
  Of scribblers who dissect my heart,
When I lie slumbering in the mould,
  Unweeting of Fame's noisy blast,
And sell for miserable gold
  The sacred secrets of the past?

To build romances from my life,
  Or weave the lies that seem like truth,
From shadows of long-ended strife
  And unknown agonies of youth?
Take them, ye flames! such fate is best;
  All but the locks of hair I crave
To wear upon my living breast,
  And perish with me in the grave!

GOOD OUT OF EVIL.

I THANK thee, O mine enemy!
  · For spiteful word and thought,
For arrowy scorn of malice born,
  And harm thou wouldst have wrought;
For by no merit of thine own,
  Or power to do me ill,
The words that from thy lips have flown
  Have falsified thy will.

Thy thoughts that would have done me wrong
  Fate read in kindlier mood,
And seeming evils turned ere long
  To unexpected good;
The drop of poison in the bowl
  Became a sweetness rare,
As clouds when riven, leave light in heaven
  And healing in the air.

Thy hand impelled with deadly force
    The missiles of thy hate,
But pitying Heaven descried their course
    And winged the bolts of Fate :
Thou wert mine enemy, God wot,
    But in the blessed end,
Each shaft at pitiless random shot
    Was guided by a friend !

AT THE CRADLE OF ROBERT BURNS.

The First Angel.

Beside the cradle where the infant slept
A pensive Angel sat—love in her mind,
And heavenly pity. Mournful watch she kept,
And sighed to think what Destiny designed
For this small morsel of humanity
That lay before her in unconscious rest,
A vernal blossom opening timidly
Its tender leaflets to the fostering west,
Unheeding of the swift approaching doom
That hovered o'er it in the stormy day
Of coming manhood, dark with lurid gloom.
" Unhappy boy!" she said. " On life's rough way,
Endowed with passions wild and judgment strong,
To keep thee right or lead thy steps astray—
Ever at war in thy tumultuous heart,
Conquerors neither! but they'll struggle long
To doubtful issues 'twixt the right and wrong,
And tempt thee to forsake the nobler part.

Cold grinding Poverty shall watch the fray
And gnaw thy vitals till thy dying day,
With all its cruel and debasing train
Of mental torture and perennial pain;
But thou shalt rise the victor o'er them all,
Lord of thy destiny, whate'er befall,
And stand erect in Fate's supremest hour,
Defying fortune and its utmost power
To quench thy proud, unyielding self-control,
Or humble thy pre-eminence of soul.
Great shall thy sorrows and thy sufferings be,
And short the span of life thy years shall see;
But in that little span, with strength innate,
Thou shalt confront unmoved the hardest fate,
And write thy name on the historic page,
Poet and wit and marvel of the age;
And dying leave thy memory to the crowd
Of all the 'unco guid' and pious proud,
Who'll scorn and scoff at, as beyond their ken,
The humble ploughman, born a king of men;
They'll note thy vices with a saintly groan,
But draw a veil discreetly o'er their own!"

SECOND ANGEL.

" Auspicious babe !" the second Angel said,
" I see the rays of glory round thy head,
And hear the unborn multitudes acclaim
In Earth's remotest climes thy honoured name !
Forlorn and sad thy path through life may be,
But high renown shall gild thy memory :
Thy words shall charm, ennoble and inspire,
And warm the popular heart with patriot fire,
And teach the poorest drudge that Fortune's ban
Cannot degrade the bravely honest man,—
And that the proud who owe their rank and state
To royal favour are but meanly great
If their nobility in deed and word
Be not inherent in the rank conferr'd,—
And that a vulgar self-sufficient churl
May call himself a Marquis, Duke, or Earl,
And fail to make himself a gentleman,
Spite of the noble fathers of the clan,
Who gave him life, though powerless to impart
Clearness of head and purity of heart ;—
This shalt thou teach in language terse and strong,
Enshrined for ever in immortal song

Sung by the teeming nations yet to be
In lands where now the savage wanders free,
But where thy gallant countrymen shall roam
In countless multitudes to find a home,
Where every man shall feel that he's a man;
'A man for a' that' in the social plan !
And happy millions shall in pride combine
To vaunt themselves as countrymen of thine—
Type of their manhood and their honest worth,
Lords of themselves and freemen of the Earth !"

THE POET'S HOPE.

I.

This Age is the age of the Mocker,
  When Reverence droops and dies,
And nothing is lovely but money
  And the vice that money buys;
How can I hope for acceptance,
  Singing an earnest song
'Mid the roar of derisive trumpets
  Bellowing loud and long?
When clowns out-value sages
  And wisdom sits forlorn,
And the lords of the popular humour
  Are apathy and scorn?

II.

How can I hope for listeners,
  When the men who think are few
If I teach that better than money
  Is the love of the good and true?

If I'd cheer the sorrow-stricken
　　Beneath the load they bear,
Or shed the light of comfort
　　On the darkness of despair?
For deaf to the song and the music
　　Are the ears of the callous crowd,
And the worshippers of Mammon
　　Are the selfish and the proud.

III.

Courage, my heart, and fear not!
　　Nor think thy fate is hard:
If to-day refuse to hear thee,
　　To-morrow may bring reward!
A steadfast hope inspires thee,
　　And shines from the far TO BE,
That a light on thy gravestone shining
　　May gild thy memory,
That the strong true heart of the people
　　May throb to hear thy name,
And that tardy recognition
　　May blossom into fame!

IV.

But if thy record perish,
　　Foredoomed, maybe, to sink

In the deep sea of Oblivion
  Wave-washed from the shelving brink,
Thy thoughts in the bright hereafter
  In the people's heart may glow,
Refining and consoling
  Alike in their joy or woe.
No truth, if great and worthy,
  Was ever taught in vain,
But shines in eternal sunshine,
  Or dies but to live again!

TWIN SISTERS.

In the same moment of that pitiless time
When earth first made its circuit round the sun,
Two sisters, different in mind and face,
Were born into the world; and they were twins,
Inseparable, but hostile each to each.
Never since then, through long millenniums pass'd,
Have they been parted; never shall they part,
Save for the breathing space that Fate allows
To the sped arrow ere it reach its mark,
As long as kings and wicked men enact
The fearful tragedies that scare the world
And plague it with untold calamities.

The elder has a smile upon her lips
And a bright sparkle in her covetous eyes,
And only lives for base and animal joys;
The younger has a face serene and sad,
Furrowed at times with melancholy wrath,
And only lives for duty to be done.

They sleep together in the selfsame bed,
They eat together at the selfsame board,
And walk together on the selfsame road;
But their minds differ, and their purposes
Are as divergent as the night and day,
The heat and cold—the wrong way and the right.

The joyous elder-born seeks not to know
What her sad sister thinks or plans or acts,
Or cares to recognise that she exists
In closest kinship with her heedless self,
But goes upon her way and works her will,
Unconscious of the footfall in the rear
Of her who follows, watchful and alert,
Close as her shadow. But the younger-born,
Stern and relentless, with a stony heart
Where awful Justice sits as on a throne,
Bides patiently her time—and then she strikes
With blow unerring as the bolts of Heaven:
The one is Crime, the other Punishment.

THE MIST AND THE STORM.

I.

Mist and cloud and humid vapours
    Lie upon the souls of men,
Dull and stifling exhalations
    Rising from a stagnant fen.
Sunshine seldom cheers their eyesight,
    Earthwards bending evermore,
Prying into filthy gutters
    For the gold that they adore:

II.

Gold which purchases the pleasures
    Their degraded nature craves—
Homage, mastery and dominion
    Over needier fools and knaves.
Power and leisure for enjoyment
    In the enervating stye
Where the sensual self-indulgers
    Grunt and wallow till they die!

III.

In the murky mist their reason
　　Is absorb'd in low desire,
Or if not extinguished wholly,
　　Grovels when it should aspire.
Deaf to rumblings of the tempest
　　Gathering o'er them unaware,
That shall burst in hail and thunder
　　And disturb and clear the air.

IV.

All the brave old-fashioned virtues
　　Shrink and shrivel to decay ;
Reverence, earnestness and honour
　　Dwindle, pine and melt away.
Slang usurps the place of language
　　Such as men and women spoke
In the days when noble England
　　Bred and trained a noble folk.

V.

Laughter fades into a giggle
　　Or the grin of dull buffoons ;
Generous thoughts are deemed a folly,
　　Love is ridiculed as " *spoons.*"

Honest wit is quenched by punning,
  Wholesome mirth is " ungenteel " ;
And success is greatly honoured
  E'en although it lie and steal.

VI.

Each inferior brainless creature,
  Simmering in his self-conceit,
With the manners of the gutter
  And the jargon of the street,
Thinks himself as good—and better
  Than the noble and the great,
And by virtue of the suffrage
  Helps to rule and wreck the State.

VII.

Liberty and Gold are idols
  Bright and fair to outward view :
Liberty for fools to govern
  All the wise and just and true,—
Gold to help them to be tyrants
  In humanity's despite,
And to buy in cheapest markets
  Wrong that passes off as Right.

VIII.

Adam Smith out-values Jesus
  In the piety of trade,
Uttering truths of greater wisdom
  Than the gospel e'er conveyed.
Jesus Christ says, "Love your neighbour;"
  Trade says, "Cheat him if you can,
Grind him, crush him and oppress him,—
  That's the method and the plan!"

IX.

This the path that leads to riches,
  All the yawning purse to fill;
Measure scant and weight deficient
  Are the helpers of the till.
Poverty's a crime detested
  By the virtuous of To-day;
All the world conspires to shun it,
  Though Hypocrisy gainsay.

X.

But the storm of vengeance rumbles
  On the fore-front of the sky;
There is conscience in the people,
  And 'twill waken by-and-by.

Many a noble tower will totter,
   Many a lofty head lie low,
Ere the storm has spent its fury;
   Woe is coming, sure, if slow!

XI.

Virtue is not dead or buried,
   It shall rouse itself anon;
Truth, though wounded, is immortal,
   And though lagging, marches on;
Sunlight, though obscure or hidden,
   Sheds from heaven its heavenly ray;
Darkness shall not last for ever;
   Storm shall sweep the fogs away!

A PREDICTION TO BE VERIFIED.

I.

Come but one burst of generous alarm,
When England's foes combine to do her wrong,
Then will our stagnant people, dull but strong,
Rise in their countless multitudes to arm!
Determined, self-reliant and blood-warm,
To guard the freedom we have cherished long!
Come but one blast of anger, that inspires
A noble nation to arise and act
And guard the heritage intact
As they received it from their valiant sires;
And Britain, mindful of a sacred fact,
Will keep alive the consecrated fires
Of wisely ordered Liberty and Right—
The world's example and its guiding light.

II.

Come but the direst storm and stress that Fate
Can bring upon us in its darkest hour,

Then will the realm awake, however late,
From the warm sloth in which we yawn and
  cower,
And pass our sordid lives in greed, or mate
With animal delights in luxury's bower:
Then will the ancient virtues bloom anew,
And love of country quench the love of gold;
Then will the mocking spirits that imbue
Our daily converse fade like misty cold,
When the clear sunshine permeates the blue
And men be manly as in the days of old,
And scorn the base delights that sink them
  down
Into the languid waters where they drown.

III.

Peace is a blessing, war may be a curse;
But peace with foul dishonour is a crime,
And when it breeds corruption, is far worse
Than war's excess, that lasts but for a time.
War is but justice, waged in self-defence,
And first of duties under wise control,
While peace maintained by coward false pretence
Is poison to the body and the soul.

The soldier fighting in his country's cause,
The trader gorging a dishonest till,
Are the two polar points of good and ill,
The Zenith and the Nadir of our laws:
Better to perish in heroic fire
Than wallow swine-like in polluting mire.

THE OLD AND NEW ORACLES.

I.

The oracles are not dumb,
The old responses come
Vaguely without control
To the inquiring soul
That humbly seeks to know
How the world-currents flow;
Dodona is not mute,
Sounds as of harp and lute
Float from the tree-tops high
As the wild wind wanders by,
And to the mind attunes
In melancholy runes
The music of the spheres
Unheard of mortal ears.

II.

The oracles, as of yore,
Whisper for evermore

To the sadly questioning brain ;
But not for ever in vain,
As the fancies of a dream
That perish ere they gleam.
In transitory light
Full on our human sight
Ever God's angels fly
Betwixt the earth and sky,
And cast from their snow-white wings
The shadows of earthly things.

III.

Still do the oracles tell
Secrets ineffable
To the spirit that would stray
Out of the bonds of clay
To search into the hidden
For knowledge unforbidden,
Except to the impure,
Unfitted to endure
The agony and stress
Of too much happiness.

IV.

The oracles as of old
Have tidings to unfold

To the unpresuming wise,
Who accept God's mysteries
Of Life and Love and Death
With firm enduring faith,
Who patiently await
At the sill of the sacred gate
To hear the anthems pour'd
In the temple of the Lord,
And the long-drawn solemn chants
Of the white-robed hierophants
Standing before the shrine
In an ecstasy divine!

V.

Faint though the oracles be
As the sigh of a placid sea,
Or the glimmer of the dawn
Ere the veil of night be drawn,
They carol in the floods,
They whisper in the woods,
They smile in the vernal flowers,
They breathe in the summer bowers,
They ripple in the streams,
They flash in the lightning gleams,

They shine in the myriad stars
From all their fiery cars,
And tell that beneath the sun
Justice is ever done,
However cruel and long
May seem the run of wrong,
And that all earth and heaven above
Live in God's land of light and love!

PERENNIAL DAISIES.

THE tender blossoms of the Spring
Fade ere the Summer birds take wing,
The Summer blooms find Autumn tombs;
But hardier daisies, bright and clear,
Gleam in the meadows all the year.

The rose that blossoms red in June,
The lily pale as young May moon,
They live their day and pass away
Before the autumnal tints appear;
But daisies blossom all the year.

The Winter storms may mar our mirth,
And with white mantle robe the earth;
But down below the sheltering snow
We find the daisies, if we peer,—
God bless the darlings of the year!

THE SWING ON THE APPLE TREE
AT FERN DELL.

I.

It stands, no beauty, on the lawn,
　　Though beautiful to me,
The rugged, crooked, gnarly, stunted
　　Blossoming apple tree.
I love to see it rich with blooms
　　As white as the feathery snow,
For it ripens thoughts as well as apples
　　Out of the long ago !

II.

Twelve summers down the gulf of Time—
　　It seems but yesterday—
I made a swing from its sturdiest boughs
　　In a morn of merry May ;
And from it swung my love, my life,
　　In the flush of her sunny youth,
And woo'd and won her to be my bride,
　　With all her love and truth.

III.

And now I swing another as fair,
　　Her years are nearly ten;
And she laughs and sings and shouts, "Papa!
　　Swing me again! again!'
And I swing her again and kiss her.
　　"Don't kick at the stars!" I cry.
And she chuckles with laughter, and says, "I will,
　　If you'll swing me up as high!"

IV.

Gnarly, crooked, rugged, wrinkled
　　Blossoming apple bough!
I do not know in the wide, wide world
　　A tree so fair as thou;
Three lives, three loves, three spirits haunt
　　Thy boughs, thou beautiful tree!
And thy fruits are the thoughts of bygone days
　　That will never return to me!

ÆOLIAN MUSIC.

O'er the loose strings of the Æolian harp
Float the wild melodies like straws on streams,—
Songs without words, but full of thoughts and
    meanings,
Though evanescent all as fancy's dreams ;
Songs of soft sadness, as if angels, weeping,
Sighed for the woes of hapless humankind,
Foredoomed to sorrow and to hopeless error,
Perverse and wayward, obstinate and blind.
I hear them at my casement, half asleep,
And weave them to my fancy as they skim
Lightly as breezes o'er a placid deep,
And fancy fashions them into a hymn,
Half praise and half lament, and melting slowly
In happy thought and tender melancholy.

A THOUGHT BY THE DEEP SEA.

I.

As I sat athinking by the deep, deep sea,
    I wished my thoughts could fly
Like autumn seeds, by the wild winds blown,
    To root beneath the sky,
Each in the fulness of the time
    To grow into a tree,
Under whose branches men might sit
    Happy and wise and free,
And war should trouble the earth no more,
    With its guilt and misery;—

II.

For if my dreams could grow into facts,
    They should run o'er the wide world's span,
And ancient lies that had governed the world
    Since Time its course began,
Should fade away in the light of day
    And cease to darken the mind,

Or harden, pervert, and lead astray
    The conscience of mankind ;
And light should pierce through dungeons' doors,
    And open the eyes of the blind.

III.

Lawyers and soldiers should lose their trade
    For want of work to be done,
And deadly struggles for daily bread
    Should cease beneath the sun ;
Food for the hungry should be as free
    As the water and the air,
Or the wholesome light of the liberal noon,
    Or the moonlight streaming fair,
And the weakest brother, no more forlorn,
    Should have a strong man's share.

IV.

Love born of knowledge should be the guide
    To lead the world aright,
And priestcraft should no more obscure
    Religion's holy Light ;
Each truth sublime that Jesus taught,
    Rejected or ignored

By more than half the teeming world,
  Despised if not abhorred,
Should in its heavenly purity
  Be followed and adored.

v.

All this should happen if my thought
  Could shape the world anew,
And make mankind forsake the false
  To reverence the true;
But if it be a barren seed,
  And only born to die,
And never fated to take root
  Under a favouring sky,
My thought is pleasant while it lasts,
  And in its light live I!

THREE GREAT WORDS:

LIBERTY—EQUALITY—FRATERNITY.

I.

LET History teach what LIBERTY has done,
As men conceive it, underneath the sun,
What shameless deeds of tyranny and wrong
Wrought on the weak by malice of the strong,
When LICENCE, wielder of the sword and flame,
Has taken Freedom's desecrated name,
And called on RAPINE, ANARCHY, and WAR
To drive o'er earth her blood-polluted car.
Word! idle word! which each man understands
In his own cause, and aids with heart and hands,
But fails to feel when others would proclaim
The right to thwart him—though the right's the same.
Freedom to think! Let centuries attest
What blood has stained the struggle and the quest
To wrench the noblest liberty of all
From grasp of priests, and worse than kingly thrall,

The rack, the stake—the agonising death,
As Roland witnessed with her dying breath.

II.

Divine Fraternity! 'tis yet unborn,
To rule, to guide, to cheer a world forlorn;
In the first dawn of Time's recorded hours
When mournful Adam quitted Eden's bowers,
And three men only walked the Earth's young sod,
Cain killed his brother for the love of God.
So in the eternal omnipresent Now,
In every region where the Fates allow
Men to exist, their frantic hosts combine
To slay their fellows for a frontier line,
For fancied wrong, for visionary right,
And seek no umpire but the arm of Might—
Might, sole reliance of the wrath of kings
Or wilder mobs, when hate or passion stings
To treat all alien peoples as their foes,
And rule and ruin all who'd dare oppose.

III.

All men are equal in the sight of Heaven
To sin and suffer and to be forgiven,
But not all equal on the teeming Earth,
Where Nature stamps diversity at birth,

Gives *this* man skill and energy to rule,
And that but wit enough to be a fool;
Gives *this* man strength to struggle to the end
And make each doubtful circumstance his friend,
And *that* man only weight enough to sink
In shallow waters on a dangerous brink!
Laws may decide all equal in their sight,
But Fate the master acts in Law's despite:
It heaves the mountain upward from the plain,
It crowns with billows the quiescent main,
And from the crowd that grovels in the mire
Raises the few and prompts them to aspire
To seize pre-eminence for good or ill
And mould the weaker fellows to their will.

Great are the Words, and worthy to be taught
To men and nations to inspire their thought;—
But though they charm the philanthropic mind,
They're dreams alone—and cheats of humankind!

A DREAM OF FAIR OCCASIONS.

I.

In the darkening shades of twilight,
　As I wandered, sore distraught,
Griefs and woes of days departed
　Surged unbidden on my thought,
Joys and sorrows intermingled
　In the memories of the Past,
Fair occasions lost and vanished,
　All too beautiful to last.

II.

Suddenly between my vision
　And the lurid setting sun
I beheld a troop of shadows
　Dimly rising one by one;
But though filmy, vague and shapeless,
　Loose and thin and undefined,
Gathering form and seeming substance
　In the rushing of the wind.

III.

Gradually in human semblance,
   Draped in robes of trailing mist,
I could trace their pallid features
   In the moonlight, now uprist;
Silently they fluttered past me,
   Each with warning hand upraised,
Long and lank and bare and skinny,
   Pointing at me as I gazed.

IV.

Well I knew them! friends and lovers
   I had scorned in days of yore,
Unobservant and ungrateful
   For the blessings that they bore:
Blessings, promises and chances
   All by kindly Fortune planned,
To be moulded to my purpose
   And be fashioned by my hand.

V.

Fortune, fame, dominion, glory,
   Friendship, love, and peace of mind,
They had brought for my acceptance
   Had I known what they designed;

But I saw not, and neglected,
  Heedless 'mid the whirl of life,
Lured by pleasure, swayed by passion,
  In the never-ending strife.

VI.

Blinded by misleading splendours,
  Prodigal of strength and youth,
Late my weary eyes were opened
  To the knowledge of the truth
That I'd wasted life's young morning
  And the noontime, past return,
Burning up the years and leaving
  Nought but ashes in the urn.

VII.

For a moment, as I sadly
  Gazed and wondered, every face
Of the pallid ghosts and phantoms
  Seemed to glow with youthful grace,
And to woo me to caress them
  As I might in life's young prime
Have caressed a radiant maiden,
  My heart's goddess for the time.

VIII.

And I called in plaintive accents,
   "Stay, ye fair ones, stay! oh, stay,
I am wiser, I am better,
   Than in youth's departed day.
I have learned from Sorrow's teaching
   Priceless truths too long unknown;
Stay and guide and shape the future,
   O my beautiful! mine own!"

IX.

Suddenly to gloom relapsing
   And evanishing from sight,
They were lost amid the darkness
   Of the melancholy night,
And I heard, as they departed,
   Fitful on the winds that bore,
Mournful voices, whispering faintly,
   "Lost! oh, lost for evermore!"

AT THE BALL AND IN THE GRAVE.

In the Ball-room.

The spring-time loveliness decays
Ere the cold autumnal days,
The petals of the lily
Fade ere the nights grow chilly,
And rose leaves fall before the year is old,
Or the gay green turns to russet gold ;
And such, alas! is living beauty's doom,
When age creeps over it to blight its bloom.

In the Grave.

But the calm beauty of the sacred dead
    Lost to our loving hearts, in life's young prime,
Remains for ever in our thought,
With tenderest recollection fraught,
    Defiant of the touch of Time,
Although the hostile seasons pass
Fond memory's magic glass,

Preserves the lovely features unimpaired,
And adds angelic grace
To the belov'd and unforgotten face
Preserved by DEATH, though LIFE would not
    have spared!

SMALL, BUT GREAT.

ONE moment in a thousand years,
  One raindrop in the sea,
One dewy daisy in the grass,
  One leaf upon the tree,
One grain of sand upon the shore,
  And in the awful sky
One planet 'mid a million suns
  That gem the galaxy,—
Are links in *One* eternal chain
  That measures Space and Time,
The greatest small—the smallest great,
  And equally sublime:
Thoughts in the infinite Mind of God,
  That knows nor great nor small,
Who formed and governs them in Love,
  And sanctifies them all!

OUR WANTS FOR THE CHILDREN.

I.

What do we want for the children ?
  We want a nobler race
Than ever since the birth of Time
  Made earth their dwelling-place.
Clear brain, fleet foot, strong hand, bright eye,
  And heart and soul and mind,
And better lives and higher aims,
  For suffering humankind.

II.

We want the fresh and flowing streams,
  Not gutters of the town—
The acorns of the living oak,
  And not the thistledown ;
We want the gold, and not the slag—
  The garden bright and fair,
And not the poisonous morass
  And the pestilential air.

III.

We want the swarming children
    To be well and wisely taught:
Not in the book of hostile creeds,
    But in the book of thought;
Not only in what mind requires,
    But what the body needs
And the State expects if it would rear
    Brave hearts for noble deeds.

IV.

All this we want for the children,—
    Self-knowledge wisely planned,
And not forlorn theologies
    Too vague to understand;
We want them to be strong and true
    In the holiness of work,
To save them from the awful streets
    Where the crime and the fever lurk.

V.

We want still more for the children,—
    We want them to be born
Of Love, not Lust that breeds and rots
    In the festering slums forlorn;

We want the fresh and wholesome shoots
  Of the orchard and the vine,
And not the stunted undergrowth,
  Or the clover for the kine.

VI.

Brave boys, good girls, for the coming years—
  'Tis these that we require,
And these we'll win though we pierce our way
  Through persecuting fire;
And though the triumph may be slow,
  The victory shall be won,
For God and man and heaven and earth
  Combine to see it done.

IN PRAISE OF DISCONTENT.

I.

Ever, for ever, without pause
　　Or change for better or for worse,
Act and react the natural laws
　　And forces of the universe;
They fill eternity and space,
　　And guide the courses of the stars;
They keep the sun in his appointed place,
　　And curb the comets in their cars.
Here, on this little crust that men call earth,
　　There's not a wind on land or sea
In all its rolling girth,
　　Or leaf that trembles on the tree,
But yields obedience to the laws divine,
Which cause the flowers to bloom, the stars
　　to shine.

II.

The laws that regulate the mind
And shape the purpose of mankind

Are universal even as they,
    And rule the human will
With irresistible sway
    For stedfast good or transitory ill.
Mighty as gravitation, that controls
    The motion of the docile spheres,
Are Love and Discontent in human souls
    To stir men's hopes and fears.
Love fills the earth with living multitudes,
    That, but for Discontent, heaven-born,
Would roam as naked in the sheltering woods
    As the wild animals forlorn,
Heedless as noontide midges on the wing
Of coming morrows and the wants they bring ;
But Discontent, the tyrant and the friend,
Plays its allotted part and destined end,
And gives weak man the strength and skill
To plough the fields and sow the seed and till
For future needs the kindly mother soil
That yields the harvests to reward his toil.

III.

'Tis Discontent that nerves his arm to slay
The ravenous beasts that hunger for their prey,

And rob them of their skins for dress
To cover and adorn his nakedness;
'Tis Discontent that guides him to the fold
For fleece to shield him from the winter cold.
Without its wholesome aid
No cities born of civilising trade
Would gem the land or tempt him to forsake
The tangled wild-wood or the sheltering brake;
No palaces or towers
 Or high cathedrals eloquent in stone
Would lift their pinnacles amid the bowers;
 No pealing organ tone,
Laden with adoration, would be heard
 Competing with the melancholy moan
Of waving wood or ocean tempest stirred;
No ships with venturous keel would sail afar
 Freighted with lofty hopes and mingling fears
In search of land beneath the southern star
 And undiscovered hemispheres,
To be in fulness of the fateful hour
The chosen centres of imperial power,
The nurseries of Science, Learning, Art,
And Piety, Religion's better part,—
All this and more, as yet concealed
From human sight, however keen its ray,

Undreamed of, unimagined, unrevealed,
Till the ripe dawn of God's appointed day
Shall yet be born of Love and Discontent
Shaped to good end, for evil never meant.

MY SEASONABLE VISITORS.

Come, childhood, come ! and banish all my sadness
  With pleasant laughter, born of artless mirth ;
Come like the spring-time in its budding gladness,
  And all the future promise of the earth.

Come, lusty manhood, looking forward ever !
  Come like the summer with its golden grain ;
Come with the genial sunshine of endeavour,
  With cooling dews and fertilising rain.

Come with the silver sprinkles in thy hair,
  Thou who art passing westward with the sun ;
Bring thy autumnal fruitage rich and rare,
  And ripened vintage of brave duty done.

Come, venerable age, with wintry head
  Calmly reposing after fitful strife,
Far onward on the path that all must tread,
  To the bright gateway of eternal life.

Come one, come all; ye are welcome to my heart,
    Whate'er the season of your years may be ;
Come to my hopeful spirit, and impart
    The warmth and light of human sympathy !

THE DOUBLE LIFE OF A RIGID SABBATARIAN.

A Portrait.

He has two souls, two consciences, two creeds,—
One, seldom used, he keeps for Sunday needs,
Like his new coat and hat and snow-white shirt,
Without a stain or speck of visible dirt;
The other serves him for his daily rule,
To keep his footing in the world's hard school,
And teach him that his pious seventh-day face
And affectation of religious grace
Need not restrain him on the other six
In lies and frauds and Trade's nefarious tricks;
And so he strives with all the strength he can
To cheat in semblance of an honest man,
And thinks it lawful for a knave to fill
His greedy pockets and remorseless till
By means unthought of in his Sunday prayers—
Short weight, short measure, and adulterate wares!

He cares not! No! not he! 'Tis gilded sin.
Let losers groan!—but let those laugh that win!
He is the winner; and when Sundays come
Goes thrice to church, looks reverently glum,
And, humbly kneeling, vows to sin no more;
But Monday sees him as he was before!

LINES.

ALL the materials are the same,
  Of blackest things and whitest,
Carbon and diamonds are but one,
And dewdrops glittering in the sun
  Are gems when they are brightest;
Base vinegar and noble wine
Are both the children of the vine;
And Love and Hate, if we but knew,
Are quite as often one, as two.

But woe is me! the bravest things
  Are commonest of any;
Much charcoal may be scattered round,
But diamond gems are seldom found,
  Though sought by very many.
Love's roses flourish on the tree
Where Hatred's thorns grow fresh and free;
The thorns are many to the view,
The roses beautiful—but few!

THE AFTERMATH.

THE first crop has been garnered,
    A crop of hopes and fears,
Of ecstasies and transports,
    And passionate sighs and tears.
It grew in fields Elysian
    In youth's delicious day,
And filled my hands with fruits and flowers,
    And all the pomps of May.

The aftermath was richer far
    In gifts of priceless worth,
Grown in the fertile places
    Of kindly Mother Earth.
It brought divine fulfilment
    To all the hopes of youth,
And sympathy in sorrow,
    And never-failing truth.

The first crop sprang in meadows,
    With clover for the kine;

The second was of purple grapes,
　To yield the noble wine;
The little germs of happy love
　That slumbered in the sod
Grew into vineyards on the hills,
　Full in the smile of God!

HATE.

Didst thou ever say "I hate"
To any man or small or great?
Retract! retract! Thou art not wise!—
If thou canst hate, disdain, despise
A child, a woman or a man,
Thy heart's to blame—thou'rt out of plan!

The sunlight falls on high and low,
And the rain rains, the rivers flow
With bounty ever large and free,
For bad and good, for land and sea:
Strive to be like them, if thou canst.
So shall thy virtues be enhanced,
If thou art virtuous, even in part,
And pure in purpose as in heart.

Hate, if thou wilt, the wrong that's wrought,
But not the doer, wrongly taught;
And in extremity of ill
Remember that he's *human* still!

THE STATUE IN THE PARK AT BRUSSELS.

THERE it stands in the mellow moonlight,
    Just as it stood in the long ago,
When I was a boy, brimful of fancies
    And passionate thoughts—Love's overflow;
My trysting-place with a fair young damsel—
    Of poor estate, I ween, was she;
But a goddess of beauty to my young fancy,
    And now—a light in my memory!

THE MIGHTY GUN AND THE LITTLE PEN.

GREAT conqueror Gun and peaceful Pen
Discourse together now and then ;—
Once in a dream, a waking trance,
By day or night—by day, perchance—
I heard them boasting, each to each,
In plain intelligible speech,
Of deeds accomplished or begun ;
And to my fancy thus spoke Gun :—

"'Tis I that rule and give the law
To keep the multitudes in awe ;
The empires of the world are mine :
I govern them by right divine,
The right of strength by Heaven decreed
To shape the will, to form the deed ;
'Tis I keep order in the realms
When civil conflict overwhelms,
And quench in blood, if needs must be,
The furious fires of Anarchy ;

I lead the nations gone astray
Back to the safe appointed way;
I keep within the bound of rules
The lust of conquerors and fools,
Who'd strew the earth with human bones,
On which to build them crazy thrones,
Did not a mightier force than theirs
Exist behind them unawares.

　　Wer't not for me the world would roll
Back in the ruts of uncontrol,
Without a master or a guide
To stem the fierce barbaric tide,
When men were wild as beasts of prey,
The naked lords of every day,
Who took no heed at set of sun
Of what the cruel day had done,
And on the morrow worked their will,
Whether to plunder or to kill,
Without a law but might and main,
Or any conscience to restrain.
I am a tyrant, understand,
But rather to be blessed than banned;
For, benefactor in disguise,
Where'er I rule I civilise."

"Thou'rt great, no doubt, when all is done,"
Said little Pen to mighty Gun;
"Thou'rt lord of how and where and when
To shape the destinies of men,
But canst not overstep thy part,
Or reason with the human heart;
Thou hast thy limits, well defined,
Thou'rt not the master of the mind.
I, little I, unseen, unheard,
Work my own wonders by a word;
I foil obstruction by a thought,
And give it wings, with lightnings fraught,
To strike the battlements of wrong,
And hurl them down, however strong.
Thy thunders perish in their birth,
Mine make the circuit of the earth,
Conversing with the time to come,
For ages after thou art dumb.
Thou buildest empires huge and high,
That flourish for a day and die,
And leave nor trace nor heritage,
Except a line on history's page,
A line, a word, a lie perchance,
For idle Rumour to enhance!

But I build empires to endure
On Truth's foundations firm and pure,
Deep laid in thoughts beyond control,
And as eternal as the soul.
In vain thy thunderbolts are hurl'd,
Thoughts are the rulers of the world,
And shape the destinies of men,—
And all *my* work!" said little Pen.

SPIN-SONG OF THE FATES.

I.

SPINNING, ever spinning,
  'Mid the moil and strife;
Spinning, spinning, spinning,—
  Such the law of life.
Swaddling clothes for new-born child,
Bridal robes for maiden mild,
Winding-sheets for Age and Pain—
Such the industrious Fates ordain,
As they turn th' eternal wheel,
  With a rush and roar,
Spinning, spinning, spinning,
  Spinning evermore.

II.

Spinning, ever spinning,
  Day and night and morrow;
Spinning, spinning, spinning
  Webs of joy and sorrow.

Warp and woof and selfsame thread
For the living and the dead.
All the patterns in the loom,
Deftly drawn by hand of Doom,
As revolves th' eternal wheel,
  With a rush and roar ;
Spinning, spinning, spinning,
  Spinning evermore !

THE MANNERS OF THE AGE.

I.

THERE's blight on the social harvest!—
　　On the women and on the men,
Blight on the little children,
　　Blight on the tongue and pen!
The blush on the cheek of beauty
　　Gives place to a stony stare,
And the eyes of the matrons utter
　　What the tongue may not declare.

II.

Men's ancient courage withers
　　In a burning thirst for pelf;
And they lose the love of virtue
　　In a baseless love of self.
The brave deeds of their fathers
　　No longer win esteem,
And float from dim remembrance
　　Like the bubbles on a stream.

III.

The minds of the little children
   Are fed on husks and straws,
Or barren stalks of logic,
   And dull scholastic laws ;
And they lose the artless credence
   That won our hearts to see,
And climb no more confiding
   To the maternal knee.

IV.

And mothers neglect to suckle
   The innocent babes they bear,
Lest they should lose enjoyment
   In the stalls of Vanity Fair,
And hand them over to hirelings
   To drain unnatural milk,
While they go flaunting and flirting
   In diamonds and in silk.

V.

Grown old before their season,
   The striplings lie' and cheat,
And talk the slang of the gutter,
   Or scrawl vile words in the street ;

And the little maids learn lessons,
    In the paths where they should not tread,
Pernicious and untimely,
    Unfit for heart or head.

VI.

The blight of the scanty knowledge
    That fancies it is great,
And flatters fools with the notion
    That they can rule the State,
Pervades the ignorant many,
    Who think they're wise as the few,
And that the false and cowardly
    Should govern the brave and true.

VII.

The pens of the ready writers
    Pollute the teeming page
With fond and foul descriptions
    Of the vices of the age ;
And the pulpits every Sunday
    Denounce the crimes of the poor,
But keep discreetly silent
    When wealth is the evildoer.

VIII.

The blight ! the blight ! the blight !
  It stretches over all ;
And the social mildew fastens
  Alike on the great or small,
Till the growing corn droops rotten
  In the fields of human thought,
And the stubble itself proves worthless,
  And the harvest comes to nought.

IX.

Must the blight endure for ever ?
  Shall the healthy storm not burst,
When the atmosphere grows heavy
  With the vapours it has nursed ?
Already the lightning flashes
  On the far horizon's cope,
And the coming tempest rumbles !—
  We watch ; and wait ; and hope !

A MODERN PHILOSOPHER.

I.

HE turns to heaven his dull grey eyes,
He opes his mouth in pompous wise,
And lets his measured accents fall,
Dull, cold and mathematical,
While he expounds his theories.

II.

He thinks he maps the human heart
With all its windings on his chart,
And knows, or fancies that he knows,
The secret source of all our woes,
And the true remedy to start.

III.

He talks of *Nature* and her laws,
Of *Man*, the *Mind*, the *Great First Cause*,
Demand, *Supply*, *Life*, *Death*, *Increase*,
The over-fruitfulness of Peace,
And argues on them clause by clause.

IV.

He thinks it time if truth were said
That mouths too many to be fed
Swarm in an over-populous land;
And that a fool might understand
That stupid peasants should not wed.

V.

He thinks it right that, for the sake
Of lands with large domains at stake,
The common people should not breed
More plenteously than they can feed,
And that coition's a mistake.

VI.

If vulgar people, boors and clowns,
And riff-raff of our teeming towns,
Would, when they mate, produce but two,
To take their place in season due,
Philosophy might spare its frown!

VII.

But, in default of this, he swears
That none should wed but rich men's heirs,
And that the common herds of man
Should eat as little as they can,
And die unmated in their cares.

VIII.

'Tis Lust, he thinks, that rules the earth,
And gives its extra millions birth;
"Is it not strange," he proudly cries,
"That I alone should be so wise
As to proclaim, for what it's worth,

IX.

"The mighty truth not taught in schools
That half the human race are fools,
And that all wisdom dwells with me
To save them from their misery,
If they'd be governed by my rules?

X.

"Alas! they grovel in dull ease,
And breed like maggots in a cheese,
And never learn that war and pest
And famine must do God's behest,
And stay their perilous increase.

XI.

"Great are my plans! I'd loose and bind
The laws of body and of mind,
And so restore the golden age
When war and pest should cease to rage
And thin the numbers of mankind;

XII.

"When men, and wiser women too,
Should curb the passions and subdue;
And calm and temperate and just,
Should make it felony to lust,
And children should be strong—but few."

XIII.

This is his dogma and pretence,
The law, he says, of Common Sense;
But yet, with wife and children blest,
He breeds for pastime like the rest,
And sternly preaches abstinence,

XIV.

And prophesies in prose and rhyme
The speedy coming of the time
When *Pestilence* in bower and town
Shall mow the human harvest down,
And *War* shall cease to be a crime!

XV.

And when, if children of the slum
In midge-like millions still should come,
Infanticide should be allowed
To ease the pressure of the crowd,
And hasten the Millennium!

XVI.

The public hoots him—nought cares he,
But pities its perversity;
Or, swathed in armour of conceit,
He warns the senate and the street
For scorning his Philosophy!

IN A THUNDERSTORM.

Let keen-eyed Science teach us what she can,
  The vast Incomprehensible confronts us still;
She strives to grope her way through Nature's plan,
  And solve the hidden mysteries at her will.
  Sitting at her window barrèd,
  She turns her glances, cold and hard,
  Up to the starry vault of heaven,
  And fancies that to her is given
  To pierce the secrets hidden from the ken
  Of the grovelling herd of men;
  But Intuition tells us more than she,
  In echoes wafted from afar
  Faintly and dimly from the infinity
  In which we float, much wondering where we are;
  There are more thoughts in Childhood's heart
  Than subtlest Reason can impart,
  Or proud Philosophy explain
  From all the heights it can attain.

So when the awful thunders crash
   Obedient to the lightning flash,
My childish faith returns; I deem I hear
The voice of God proclaiming from the sphere
   That Retribution follows Crime
   In its due appointed time,
Slow and precarious though it seems to be
To our weak eyes, that cannot see
Beyond the limits of the hour
That comes and goes ere we have felt its power
To shape to-morrow's purpose through the gloom,
That hides the coming certainty of doom.

There are far deeper lessons in the soul
Than Science can presume to teach
   By rule and logical control,
   However loftily they preach.
Cling to me, O ye instincts of my youth!
Shadows, it may be, of Eternal Truth!

BLESSINGS IN DISGUISE.

Milton and Beethoven.

I.

Milton sits musing in the porch,
  The bright blue sky above him;
But cannot see the light of Heaven,
  Or smiles of those who love him.
But though the utter darkness hides
  The earthly from his vision,
He sees the bowers of Paradise
  And splendours of the Elysian;
He learns from angels at his side
  Creation's awful story,
And looks upon them face to face,
  Undazzled by their glory.

II.

Beethoven—Music's great high-priest,
  Whose heaven-born fancies capture

The tangled skeins of harmony ·
  And weave them into rapture—
Hears not the voice of humankind,
  Nor sound of life or motion,
Nor tempests on the echoing hill,
  Nor moan of restless ocean;
And yet in silence of his mind
  Can hear the throb and thunder
Of jubilant hymns and solemn chants,
  And lays of love and wonder.

III.

Thus, though relentless Fate may close
  The gateways of our senses,
Immortal spirit overleaps
  Its barriers and defences,
And with celestial recompense
  For harm and loss diurnal
Yields greater joy than Flesh affords,—
  A foretaste of th' Eternal:
To blind old Milton's rayless orbs
  The light divine is given,—
And deaf Beethoven hears the hymns
  And harmonies of heaven!

THE TWO SLAIN GENERALS.

I.

In the cold and drear December,
  In the waning of the night,
A vision passed before me
  By the dim, uncertain light :
A vision of hosts and armies
  Battling for wrong—or right.

II.

Ten times ten thousand warriors
  Were ranged on either side,
In squadrons and battalions
  Deploying far and wide ;
Ghosts of departed heroes
  That had bled and fought and died.

III.

Dull in the mist, their banners
  Hung hueless every one ;

There came no breath of sulphur
  From the jaws of the murderous gun,
And the swords and spears and rifles
  Were shadowless in the sun.

IV.

It seemed as if legion to legion
  Inquired with anxious eyes,
Why did we hate each other?
  How did this strife arise?
And why did this misery happen
  Under God's holy skies?

V.

The serried ranks reopened
  In dim and dark array,
And the pale ghost of a hero
  Slain in the fateful fray,
Astride on a spectral charger,
  Stood forth in the dawning day.

VI.

And from the opposing phalanx
  Another, like to him
In shadowy form and feature
  And resolute eye and limb,

As if leading hosts to battle,
  Loomed large in the fog-light dim.

VII.

And the one said to the other,
  " General, we died in vain
In the quarrel which we sought not ;
  And the blood of thousands slain
Cries up to outraged Heaven
  From the gory battle-plain.

VIII.

" Brother in crime and sorrow,
  Brother in fearful wrong,
The foolish crowd exalt us
  With plaudits loud and long,
And chant our praises daily
  In sermon and in song.

IX.

" They call us great and mighty,
  Because by passion led
We sought to gather glory
  In the vineyards of the dead,
And cared not for the rivers
  Of innocent blood we shed ;

X.

" Because we rushed to battle
  To struggle in a cause
That might have marched to triumph
  Amid the world's applause,
If men had been obedient
  To God's eternal laws."

XI.

" Ay," said his brother warrior,
  "The victory was not worth
The smoke of the powder wasted
  In heralding its birth,
Or the blood of the meanest soldier
  That sank into the earth:

XII.

" But man is a cruel tyrant,
  The foe of his brother-man ;
Pitiless and remorseless,
  By impulse and by plan,—
Is, and for ever has been,
  Since Time its course began,

XIII.

"On all who strive to thwart him
  In the frenzy of his need,
In his hunger of dominion,
  In his hate of a rival creed,
Or love of a neighbour's frontier,
  That tempts his selfish greed.

XIV.

"And we became his hirelings,
  And pandered to his lust,
Helping to wreak his vengeance,
  Unreasoning and unjust,
On our offending brothers,
  And harmless fellow-dust.

XV.

"Let us be friends, my brother."
  And I saw, with moistening eyes,
That they clasped their hands together
  As the mists began to rise,
And the shadowy legions vanished
  In the light of the morning skies.

ON THE PLACE DE LA CONCORDE, PARIS.

I.

Lone wandering through the street
With desultory feet,
Led by wild fancies idly to and fro,
I lingered on the square
So awful yet so fair,
Misnamed of Concord, where no concords grow:
The founts had ceased to play,
The mist hung dark and grey,
And clad the spectral trees, like mourners robed
for woe.

II.

Upon the Seine's dark breast
The ripples were at rest—
There blew no wind to curl them on the stream;
The city was asleep,
The very mist did creep

As if 'twere drowsy, and each lamp's dim beam,
    Athwart the dreary night,
    Shone out with nebulous light,
Ring-circled, vague and thick—a melancholy gleam.

III.

    Whole phalanxes of ghosts,
    In long-drawn shadowy hosts,
Headless and horrible, usurped the ground,
    That seemed alive with Death;
    Without a sigh or breath
To break the pulseless quietude around,
    In the cathedral tower
    The solemn midnight hour
Shook, whispering with a faint and muffled sound.

IV.

    I saw before me pass,
    As in a magic glass,
A mournful spectre looming through the haze;
    Upon his brow he wore
    The semblance, red as gore,
Of a king's crown, the gaud of other days,
    Such as might well beseem
    The glory and the dream
Of lost dominion and the people's praise.

V.

Where Luxor's giant stone
Stands awful and alone
A scaffold reared its grim revengeful head ;
And round its basements rude
A fearful multitude
Of fitful ghosts, neither alive nor dead,
Paced to the throb and thrum
Of the monotonous drum
In slow funereal march and melancholy tread.

VI.

And lo ! before my sight,
In gleams of lurid light,
I could discern, as in a palimpsest,
The wearer of the crown
Kneel reverently down,
With pious hands enfolded on his breast,
While from his lips a prayer,
Borne on the stagnant air,
Implored of pitying Heaven the boon of blessed
rest.

VII.

The blessing was conferr'd,
The mournful prayer was heard,

The deed was done, the thread of life was riven;
>While a voice, calm and low,
>Hopeful, but full of woe,
Said, " Patience, brother! be thy sins forgiven;
>Angels attend on thee,
>Death is great victory!
" Son of Saint Louis, find thy home in Heaven!"

FAILURES.

Millions of germs never grow into life,
    On the land or in the sea;
Millions of acorns fall to the ground
    And never produce a tree;
Millions of people live and die
    On Earth's prolific breast,
But scarcely produce in a thousand years
    A man above the rest,
To guide them into higher life
    Than ever before they knew,
To lead them out of the false and bad
    Into the good and true.
And when he comes they heed him not,
    Or if they heed, they slay
For being wiser than themselves
    And born before his day!

THREE DECEIVERS.

I.

WHEN I was young, in lusty health,
    Two visions floated o'er me,—
The one was *Fame*, the other *Wealth*,
    And bright the shore before me,
Fair glittering in the morning ray.
But ere the noon of youthful day
A phantom lovelier than they
    Stood radiantly beside me.
It whispered music, day and night,
Its smiles were more than noonday bright,
Its eyes were fountains of delight
    To comfort and to guide me!

II.

'Twas *Love*, with witchery on her tongue,
    Who from her lustrous glances
Whole sheaves of feathered arrows flung,
    Well sharpened with romances.

She lured and led me from the bowers,
And promised me more blissful hours
Than Fame or Wealth and all their dowers
    Could yield, and never vary.
Alas! I yielded to the thrall
Of each in turn—in rise and fall—
And found they were impostors all,
    To cheat the heart unwary!

III.

Fame brought Detraction in his train,
    And Envy strove to spite me,
While Wealth, acquired in toil and pain,
    Was powerless to delight me.
Love, though a traitor, like the rest
Was far the pleasantest and best,
And gave my life a nobler zest
    Than either of her rivals;
And so, if victim I must be,
The least unworthy of the three
Shall hold my foolish heart in fee,
    The last of the survivals!

HOW MANY AND HOW FEW.

I.

How many raindrops fall in the river,
How many rays in the sunshine quiver,
How many lovers' vows are broken,
How many lies are daily spoken,
How many knaves in the morning rise,
How many fools are thought to be wise,
How many leaves are on the tree,
How many gallons in the sea,
And how many sorrows oppress the men
Who live to threescore years and ten?

II.

Hard to reckon! Easier far
To count how few the happy are,
Or the vows in Love's bright summer made
That are truly kept in the wintry shade,
Or the hopes of youth in its blossoming May
That ripen to fruit in the autumn day,

And the hearts that after years of pain
Would choose to live their lives again ;
Easy to count them if we knew,—
O Life, be Love! O Love, be true!

THE SECRET.

I.

I FOUND a secret long ago,
 Before I'd passed my middle prime,
To turn a friend into a foe,
 And blunt the shafts of hostile Time.

II.

To revel in my youthful thought,
 When cruel age was creeping on ;
And sail Life's ship with fancies fraught
 O'er seas where placid summer shone.

III.

How I could bathe in fountains fair
 For hope and love and healing meant,
And breathe the soft and balmy air
 Of gratitude and sweet content.

IV.

How I could keep my wayward heart
 Pure as a child's in its morn of life,

Nor suffer courage to depart,
    Or perish in the moil and strife.

V.

How not to creep, but to aspire;
    How to widen my narrowing ken;
How keep alive the sacred fire
    Of love to God and my fellow-men.

VI.

Yes! I discovered it long ago—
    The little secret--so large to bless,
That lightened the load of every woe,
    And robed the world in loveliness.

VII.

Wouldst know the secret? Short to tell:
    You cannot read it in my looks.
I found it where it loves to dwell,
    In the noblest and the best of books:

VIII.

In the holy Sermon on the Mount,
    In poet's page of lofty truth;—
These were the waters of the Fount,
    These the renewers of my Youth!

SONNET.

Could we but know, and, knowing, durst proclaim
   How much the thoughts of an exultant youth
   Owe to the promptings of eternal Truth
Infused into our souls like living flame,
The cold and callous world would scorn and blame,
   Or look upon us with a dull surprise,
   And call us mad for seeming to be wise
Beyond our years, and bid us hush for shame.

Alas! we know not, till in after time
Too late to profit by, too fitful bright;
   Though wild and vague, too near to the sublime,
Were the ennobling thoughts by Fancy drawn
   Unwittingly for Heaven to give us light
In the fresh sunrise of our mortal dawn!

WHAT THE MORNING SUN SAID TO THE FLOWERS.

Ye happy, beautiful and innocent things,
　God's only angels in a world of pain,
Angels in all except the snowy wings
　To float and soar o'er heaven's eternal plain,
Sin casts no shadow o'er your radiant faces,
And grief avoids your holy dwelling-places;
Ye live, ye love, ye propagate and die,
And ope your joyous petals to the sky,
Rose-red and lily pale and heavenly blue,
And bask in my warm beams from morns till eves,
To drink the cooling moisture of the dew
That freshens and sustains your drooping leaves;
Your lives are free from sorrow, sin and care,
And ye are happy knowing ye are fair—
Happier than birds or beasts or humankind
Or insects, happier still than all that wage
Insensate wars with instinct fierce and blind
Against their fellow-creatures, to assuage

The cruel and relentless hunger-pains
That rouse their passions and inflame their veins;
But ye! ye innocent nurslings of my rays,
Live purer lives and sanctify the earth,
Which ye adorn by your perennial birth
And generous loveliness of summer days,
When ye display your beauties to the light
In manifold glories to man's grateful sight.
Ye break no laws, ye live unsullied hours,
And feel no pangs of sorrow in the bowers,
Inflicting none! and only spreading pleasures
To all who prize your ever-teeming treasures.
Born of my beams, I love you every one,
Gems of the earth and darlings of the sun!

CIRCLES.

ALL the worlds exist in circles;
  In a circle blows the wind,
In a circle flows the life-blood,
  And in circles acts the mind:
On and on, and on for ever,
  Travelling east we reach the west;
Suns and galaxies and systems
  All obey the same behest,
Never swerving into tangents,
  Never passing into rest.

Everything in God's creation,
  Guided by a law Divine,
Is imprisoned in a circle,
  And knows nothing of a line.
God alone extends for ever
  Through the past infinity,
Through the present to the future,
  Is and was and is to be—
Lives unending, unbeginning,
  Mystery of mystery!

ELOGE DE LA FOLIE.

Not BY ERASMUS.

I.

SOME sing of wisdom and its charms
    In tuneful melancholy,
But I will choose another theme,
    And sing the praise of Folly.
Folly's the ruler of the world,
    As history evinces;
The bosom friend, the confidant
    And counsellor of princes.

II.

When statesmen meet in senate halls
    To plan the fate of nations,
Close at their elbows Folly flits
    To shape their disputations.
It whispers in their willing ears,
    Unseen and unsuspected,
And shapes their actions into forms
    Which Wisdom had rejected.

III.

There's not a potentate on earth
  So .mighty in dominion
As Folly, master of the wise
  And tyrant of opinion.
'Tis Folly keeps the world alive
  In all its generations,
And sits as arbiter of fate
  And umpire of the nations.

IV.

'Tis Folly makes us fall in love
  When health and youth run riot,
And keeps the bright steel blade of mind
  From mouldiness and quiet;
'Tis Folly makes us rush to war
  And pour out blood like water,
And all for glory and renown
  To be acquired by slaughter.

V.

'Tis Folly makes the wine-cup flow
  When joyous comrades revel,
And drags the stupid and the wise
  Down to a common level ;

'Tis Folly shouts hip, hip! hurrah!
　　With voice enthusiastic,
When lies come rattling from the tongue
　　In praise encomiastic.

VI.

'Tis Folly makes us think that gold
　　All other good surpasses,
And value the applause of crowds
　　Though it be brayed of asses;
'Tis Folly that depends on luck,
　　And not upon endeavour,
To feed the fires of enterprise
　　And keep them hot for ever.

VII.

'Tis Folly makes the millions cheer
　　By self-sufficient warrant,
When statesmen gifted with the "gab"
　　Pour out their windy torrent,
And take five weary hours to tell
　　What might be better ended
In twice five minutes, with less risk
　　To common-sense offended.

VIII.

'Tis Folly wakes the slumbering world
   And sets it briskly going,
And keeps life's fashionable stream
   For ever fresh and flowing.
So long live Folly! guide of man
   Since time's remotest ages,
The sovereign of the multitude
   And mentor of the sages!

POPULARITY.

He hit the bad taste of the silly and thoughtless,
  The silly and thoughtless rewarded him well;
The critics encored him, the maidens adored him—
  Whatever he published was certain to sell.
The multitude bought him, the publishers sought
    him,
  Who could compare with him ? Who could excel ?

One who excelled him by ten times ten thousand,
  Sang for the wise and the good and the true;
Thought them majority, found them minority,
  Friendly and loving, but hopelessly few.
How could he count with his butcher and baker ?
  How could he live upon sunshine and dew ?

The bard of the silly splashed by in his chariot —
  His was the homage and *his* the acclaim ;

The bard of the thoughtful trudged by in the gutter,
  And looked to the future for profitless fame.
What does it signify?—Man can but live and
  die :
  Living, he's nobody ; dead, he's a Name !

KILLING THE TIME.

I.

KILL Time? And why should I kill him?
  I want him to be my friend,
To live with him and cherish him
  In the fast-approaching end;
To roam with me in the wild wood,
  To pluck the wayside flowers,
Or sit with me and my loved one
  In the leafy summer bowers.

II.

Kill Time? But why should I kill him,
  My friend all friends beside,
When he can teach me wisdom
  To comfort me and guide,
When he can strew my pathway
  With lily and thyme and rose,
And lilac and laburnum,
  And any blossom that grows?

III.

Kill him? Why should I kill him,
  In the sight of the chiding sun,
In ignorant self-slaughter,
  When he and my life are one,
When kindly Heaven deputes him
  To cheer me on the road,
Not darksome altogether,
  That leads me up to God?

IV.

Kill him? Ah, no! I'll bless him,
  And study him all I can:
He's not my foe, nor ever was
  Through all his little span;
He brings me gifts from day to day,
  And 'mid the moil and strife
Of the busy world, where Death is lord,
  He holds me on to life.

V.

'Twould be ungrateful and unjust
  If I should do him wrong,
And, though when oft I think him short,
  He seems perversely long:

The fault lies wholly with myself,
   And Time is not to blame,
Who holds his course, through good and ill,
   Eternally the same.

VI.

'Tis true that by all-wise decree
   He ripens young to old,
And dims the light of beaming eyes,
   And turns the warmth to cold;
But that's no reason we should haste
   The inevitable day,
By killing him whose life is ours:
   I'll use him while I may!

THE OLD TREE.

There's life in the old tree yet:
　　It opens its buds to the spring,
And rustles its leaves to the soft west wind,
　　When the lark and the nightingales sing;
It yields the owl a sheltering rest,
　　And the bright-eyed squirrel a run,
And casts a shade on the mossy sward
　　Under the noonday sun,—
A shade where weariness may rest
　　And indolence may dream,
And sweethearts carve their names on the bark,
　　And muse on the joy supreme.

There's life in the old tree yet
　　To brave the wintry storm,
And pith in its wide-extended roots
　　To keep its branches warm;
So let the wild winds blow their worst,
　　Come frost, come hail, come rain,

Come anything but the lightning stroke
And the weird, wild hurricane,—
The tree shall stand for its destined hour,
And bloom in the spring again !

ONLY STRAWS!

The Devil sat at the dawn of day,
Amid the crowds on a broad highway,
By the bank of a mighty river,
That dashed and foamed and rolled for ever,
With waves and winds and constant strife—
The dark and treacherous River of Life.

The teeming people on the shore,
Wistfully watching evermore,
Gazed on the straws that the Devil cast
Into the torrent hurrying past,
And with impatient hand and eye,
As the worthless waifs went floating by,
Strove to catch them in eager haste,
Wading naked from the waist,
Or in defiant strength and pride
Leap'd all headlong into the tide,
To seize the straws by the tempter flung
To dazzle and cheat the old and young,

The weak, the strong, the shy, the bold,
By wisps of visionary gold.

I asked, unknowing what to think,
A keen spectator on the brink,
What caused the madness of the crowd.
" Madness ? " he answered me aloud;
" They are not mad, but brave and wise:
They know the value of the prize !
Straws, did you say ? They're great rewards,
The best that kindly Earth affords;
They're wealth, dominion, power and fame,
More precious than the tongue can name.
Who gains them makes the world his own,
And sits like monarch on a throne,
To tower above the common herd,
Supreme in action and in word !"

He ceased and, darting from my side,
Sprang exulting in the tide;
Young he was and fair to see,
And confident of victory,
And 'mid the waters deep and vast
Clutched at every straw that passed;
And though at times he gasped for breath,
He feared no conqueror but Death,

And in the struggle took no heed
Of his competitors in greed,
Who pressed upon him all around :
He strove, he struggled, and he drowned,
And sank with faint expiring groan
Down to the bottom like a stone!

His stronger rivals stepped ashore—
Pale-faced, dim-eyed, and wearied sore,
Old and decrepid ere their time,
Or foul of feet with slush and slime,
To flaunt the straws which they had won
Triumphant to the noonday sun,
Or hug them proudly to their breasts,
And wear like trophies in their crests.

Alas! I thought, that men should be
Such dupes and victims as to see
A treasure in the worthless straws
That win their worship and applause ;
That in their greed they should despise
God's choicest blessings to the wise—
Health, strength, and blessed peace of mind,
And love, best boon of humankind !
Alas! that they should sell their souls
For paltry and deluding doles,

And shadowy dreams of wealth and power,
That cheat them for a fretful hour,
And veil from their defrauded sight
The glories of the Infinite,
And send them to the grave forlorn
To weep that they were ever born,
Poor little wormlings of the sod,
That creep and crawl, and know not God!

GUTTERSLUSH:

Maker of Parliaments.

I.

Gutterslush, one of the million,
  Can neither read nor write,
But can drink and swagger and bluster,
  And, if he likes, can fight.
He labours for his daily bread,
  And thinks the toil severe;
And spends the better half of his wage
  In tobacco and in beer.

II.

His wretched, ragged helpmate
  Works harder far than he,
To earn a crust for the starving brats
  That clamber at her knee
Or swarm in the putrid alleys
  In the puddle and the rain,
To pluck up vice in the gutter,
  Deadening heart and brain.

III.

And Gutterslush is a voter
  By right of the rent he pays,
Or allows his life's poor partner
  To hoard for the evil days,
When the landlord of their dog-hole
  Might turn them into the street,
To howl for coppers to purchase drink
  On pretence of bread to eat.

IV.

And Gutterslush *thinks* he's a "thinker,"
  Because of the paltry vote,
That he'd sell to the highest bidder,
  If only for a groat,
To buy the beery poison
  Or the throat-inflaming gin,
And think no shame of the bargain,
  But clinch it with a grin.

V.

Is he not one of the million
  That help to rule the State?
And choose the men of action—
  The brave, the true, the great,

And aid it to hold the position
  It held in days bygone,
When wisdom sat at its councils
  And guarded the steps of the throne;

VI.

When fools and knaves and cowards
  Were ruled, but did not rule,
And the teachers were not governed
  By the dunces of the school;
When the doctors, not the patients,
  Kept peace in Bedlam's halls,
And the warders, not the felons,
  Were the lords in the prison walls?

VII.

Gutterslush looks at the windows
  Of the all-too-tempting shops,
Where the glittering watches dangle,
  And the diamonds hang in drops
Or gloats at the sight of the bacon
  That might exercise his jaw,
If he had not to work and win it
  Ere it reached his greedy maw.

VIII.

Every man is a foeman
  (In Gutterslush's eye,)
Who wears a better coat on his back
  Than idleness can buy.
And Gutterslush as a voter
  Is great on election day,
When a party-ridden nation
  Indulges in its craze ;

IX.

And accepts the voice of the many
  As an oracle divine,
Though the voice be as void of reason,
  As the rowt and roar of kine—
The mob that is bound to labour,
  And has not leisure to think,
And traders engrossed in trading
  Hear nought but the money's chink.

X.

Or, closely packed together
  In the grip of the teeming town,
Strive in their desperation
  · To trample each other down,

And goaded by fear of hunger,
   Limit their little skill,
To sell by fraudulent measure,
   And the filling of the till.

XI.

And scruple not to poison
   The unoffending poor,
By the carrion food they sell them ·
   At a profit large and sure,
To be got from the ready penny
   In a famishing woman's hand,
Who has sold, perchance, her virtue
   For the pence at her command.

XII.

The Gutterslushes rule us,
   And surge and overwhelm
The buttresses and bulwarks
   Of a once majestic realm ;
And take no heed of the rivals,
   Many and brave and strong,
That are springing up around us
   As the swift years hurry along.

XIII.

And, alas! our would-be statesmen,
　　Floundering in faction's mire,
Will walk as their party bids them,
　　Though it lead through flood and fire;
Not giving a thought to duty,
　　Or their suffering country's need
Of honest men to rule it,
　　In all their thought and deed.

XIV.

If Gutterslush were but One,
　　Small evil might be wrought;
But he's part of a swarming million,
　　Unscrupulous and untaught,
Though he knows the gospel of greed
　　And every man for himself,
And the devil take the hindmost
　　In the dastardly struggle for pelf!

XV.

But the million are the masters
　　Till the destined end shall come,
And the court and the camp and the forum
　　Shall be captured by the Slum:

Demos is lord and monarch
  Supreme in bower and town,
With a firebrand for a sceptre
  And a fool's cap for a crown !

XVI.

And Jack is as good as his master,
  And Jill is the quean of the land,
And covers the streets with her children
  To shame us where we stand.
Vox Populi!   Vox Stultorum!
  Are they not the same—
Speaking in tones of thunder
  And devastating flame ?

OH FOR A MAN !

Oh for a man of soul sublime
To dwarf the pigmies of our time,
Of honest and far-reaching mind,
Who sees his way to loose and bind,—
A man to act, and not to spout
His weary floods of mazy doubt,
And flux of words in dark disguise
To vex the patience of the wise.

Oh for a man of heart and hand,
The guiding spirit of the land,
To keep intact from knaves and fools
And slavish bigots of the schools
The glorious privileges won
And handed down from sire to son,
That made our Britain stand erect,
A model for the world's respect,
The friend of right, th' oppressor's dread,
The heart of freedom and its head !

Oh for a man to write his name
Clear on the luminous scroll of fame,
A man of purpose, strength and wit,
Like brave old Palmerston and Pitt,
To foil the cowardly of To-day,
Who seek to squander and betray
For sake of petty power and gold
The glorious heritage of old !

Oh for a man ! He'll come ! he'll come !
To strike our garrulous drivellers dumb,
And prove that patriot virtues still
Inspire the heart and guide the will
Of statesmen worthy of the name
To vindicate their country's fame,
And lift her glorious banner high,
Defiant of the stormiest sky,
To breeze and blast alike unfurl'd,
A signal to th' expectant world !

WEALTH UNTOLD

SEEK for treasure, and you'll find
It exists but in the mind.
Wealth is but the power that hires
Blessings that the heart desires;
And if these are mine to hold
Independently of gold
And the gifts it can bestow,
I am richer than I know.

Rich am I, if when I pass
Amid the daisies on the grass,
Every daisy in my sight
Seems a jewel of delight!
Rich am I, if I can see
Treasure in the flower,and tree,
And can hear 'mid forest leaves
Music in the summer eves;
If the lark that sings aloud
On the fringes of the cloud

Scatters melodies around
Fresh as rain-drops on the ground,
And I bless the happy bird
For the joy it has conferr'd ;
If the tides upon the shore
Chant me anthems evermore ;
And I feel in every mood
That life is fair and God is good!
I am rich if I possess
Such a fund of happiness,
And can find where'er I stay
Humble blessings on the way,
And deserve them ere they're given
By my gratitude to Heaven !

ON THE DUOMO OF MILAN.

I.

On Milan's high cathedral towers,
   Amid the marble saints I stand,
And look beneath upon the bowers
   Far spreading of the glorious land
Sublimely fair. On every side
   The splendours rise, the beauties glow—-
The leafy plains in summer's pride—
   The mountain summits robed in snow.

II.

But 'tis not Nature's lovely face
   That here shall captivate the mind;
Man is the genius of the place,
   And claims the homage of his kind.
E'en as on Alpine peaks I gaze,
   The hoary guardians of the clime,
I think the thoughts of other days,
   And dream the dreams of future time.

III.

I deem, if voice of theirs could speak,
    What deeds their thunders might recall,
What wrongs of Roman and of Greek,
    What crimes of Vandal and of Gaul;
What seas of blood in warfare spilt,
    What hecatombs of heroes slain,
What ruthless misery and guilt,
    What myriad battles, fought in vain.

IV.

O Italy ! superbly fair !
    O matron, beautiful and chaste !
To wanton with thy raven hair,
    And loose the girdle from thy waist,
The kings and robbers of the world,
    Have fought and wrestled evermore,
And only kiss'd thy lips impearl'd,
    To stain thy lovely breast with gore !

V.

With mangled limbs and bleeding head
    Chain-bound in many an iron coil,
Death-smitten wert thou ! but not dead—
    A prize for ruffians to despoil;

Ruffians impervious to remorse,
    Enthralled and haunted by thy charms,
Who'd rather trample on thy corpse
    Than yield thee to another's arms.

VI.

Brave Italy! thou couldst not die!
    Thy sons, beneath their tyrants' yoke,
Looked up to God's benignant sky
    With faith that never failed—or broke;
They revelled in the realms of thought,
    And dared oppression to subdue
The love they felt, the truths they sought
    In Art and Science—old or new.

VII.

They raised in Dante's grasp sublime
    The blazing torch of epic song;
Taught Tasso the heroic rhyme
    For after ages to prolong:
Taught Michael Angelo to wield
    The magic brush that witch'd mankind,
And forced the marble block to yield
    The gods and goddesses of mind.

VIII.

They filled the world with fairer forms
  Than dull reality supplies,
Except to those whom Fancy warms
  To gaze with sympathetic eyes;
And gave to Europe, trodden low
  Beneath the heels of armèd men,
A·light to lead it—and to show
  How it might rise to life again.

IX.

By KNOWLEDGE, POETRY and ART,
  And UNION under wise control,
In field and town and trading mart,
  To crush the despots of the soul,
Wear them as ·waters wear the rocks
  When ocean tides their strength assail,
And not by fitful earthquake shocks,
  Or flying storms of sleet and hail.

X.

And not in vain—though PRIEST and KING
  And wily statesmen did their best
To stop the waters at the spring—
  They gushed and overflowed the West.

And Europe bathing in the flood
  Drank freedom from the healing tide,
And won through agony and blood
  The rights the robber had denied.

XI.

And Italy—itself at last,
  After long struggles stood erect,
Freed from the bondage of the Past,
  From wrong—from outrage—from neglect;
Shone forth a gem in Europe's crown
  A priceless jewel, set in gold,
With youthful fire and proud renown,
  To light the nations as of old.

XII.

Thoughts are the rulers of the world,
  And weave the texture—warp and woof,
Of Rights from banner high unfurled—
  And Truth's white robes—destruction-proof;
Such are the thoughts with which I burn
  Long musing on the Duomo's cope;
Such is the lesson that I learn
  For men and nations—WORK and HOPE!

WRITING AND PUBLISHING.

I AM not wrong, you say, to write—
- But wrong to publish: no one needs
The songs and poems I indite,
    And no one cares for them or reads.
What does it matter, I reply?
    The mavis on the hawthorn bough
And lark on forehead of the sky
    Sing not to expedite the plough!
They scatter melody like rain
    Bursting in freshness from the cloud,
And care not though they chant in vain,
    Unknown, unheeded of the crowd.
They sing for casement of their heart,
    And I for mine, in every tone;
My song's my life, my better part—
    My joy, my comfort, and mine own!

A NEW BALLAD WITH AN OLD BURDEN.

I.

WHEN this old cap was new—
  'Tis eighty years ago—
There was elbow room in the land
  Both for the high and low,
There were hope and scope for all
  Who could wisely think and do
And take the world as they found it,
  When this old cap was new.

II.

Reverence dwelt in the thought
  Of the young man for the old,
And age was accounted honour,
  Even if lacking gold.'
Money was not the god,
  But the servant of the true,
And held in trust for the people,
  When this old cap was new.

III.

Workmen did honest work
  To earn an honest fee,
And none thought labour a curse
  Whatever a man's degree,
Sons respected their fathers,
  Daughters their mothers too,
And their love was very lovely,
  When this old cap was new.

IV.

"Ladies" were seldom heard of,
  But abounded all the same,
And were known as "gentlewomen,"
  And worthy of the name ;
They did not live to dress
  And flirt with nothing to do,
Or to squander the time in shopping,
  When this old cap was new.

V.

No "gentleman" in their presence
  Was rude enough to smoke,
Or utter a too suggestive word
  In earnest or in joke ;

Or address them in casual meeting
Even with a "*How d'ye do?*"
Except with head uncovered,
When this old cap was new!

VI.

The vulgar slang of the street
    Was to the street confined,
And never found an utterance
    On the lips of the refined;
But was left to the slums and stables,
    And to tramps and the cadging crew,
Who knew no other language,
    When this old cap was new.

VII.

A servant girl was a servant,
    And was not called a "miss,"
But Jane or Sarah or Mary Ann,
    As the fashion no longer is;
And did not ape her mistress
    In pink or green or blue,
But dressed in sober garments
    When this old cap was new.

VIII.

The little children frolicked
  In the garden or the mead,
And believed in fairy stories
  In thought and word and deed,
Respected Jack and the Beanstalk
  And Sindbad the Sailor true,
And never heard of an "'ology"
  When this old cap was new!

IX.

A trader's word was his bond,
  And if he measured an ell,
'Twas an ell to the shade of an inch
  Either to buy or sell;
Butter was churned from milk,
  And malt and hops were in brew,
And wine was made from the actual grape
  When this old cap was new!

X.

The "gift of the gab" was a blemish
  In those who aspired to rule,
And was not the test of a statesman,
  But oftener of a fool;

Deeds, and not words, were the proofs
Of wisdom tried and true
In the councils of the nation,
When this old cap was new!

XI.

The land was not encumbered
With paupers lacking bread,
And the guardians of the poor
Had heart as well as head;
The prisons had cells to spare,
And the inmates were but few,
For work was not starvation
When this old cap was new!

XII.

Betting was not a business,—
Races were fairly run;
And melancholy jokers
Had mercy in their fun,
And did not pump up ancient jests
In journal or review
To prove what absolute fools they were
When this old cap was new!

XIII.

Men met in the social circle
    When the wine and the wit were poured,
And hospitality flourished
    E'en at the poor man's board;
All intercourse was courteous
    Between the many and few,
And the world was all the better,
    When this old cap was new!

XIV.

But care and money-grubbing,
    And the pressure of the crowd,
And "Devil take the hindmost"
    Shouted aloft and aloud,
Have hardened the heart and the manners,
    And driven the world askew,
Since the happier days departed,
    When this old cap was new!

A VERY GREAT KING.

I.

A KING! a King! a mighty King!
  Who rules unquestioned Lord,
More potent than an·emperor,
  A tyrant—but adored!
King HUMBUG governs countless realms
  More populous by far
Than ever fell to cruel stroke,
Or bent beneath the hardest yoke
  Of conqueror in war.

II.

The Attilas and Charlemagnes,
  Who slaughtered fresh and free,
Or sat on thrones of human bone,
  Were feebler far than he;
For HUMBUG cares not to destroy,

But, merciful to men,
He rules them in a softer guise,
By smiles and tricks and frauds and lies
And skill of tongue and pen.

III.

And yet, perchance, if we could count
The harm that he has done,
And daily does in every realm
Beneath the blessed sun,
We might confess that gun and sword
Were easier to control
Than Humbug, with his false pretence,
Who spares our bodies but to fence
His treason to the soul.

IV.

So long live Humbug! Mighty king!
Who rules without a peer,
The head and master of the world,
To all his subjects dear;
Though wars may cease, yet long as men
Are easier to kill
Than to be forced to love the truth,
He'll flourish in immortal youth,
Obeyed and worshipped still!

ANCIENT ERRORS.

Lives there a man who hopes to slay
An ancient error in our day?
Let him attempt it if he will,
And work, and work, and work his fill:
He'll find, when he has struck a blow,
How weak his arm, how strong his foe,
And that against its brazen mail
The sharpest lance will not avail!
If, reeling from the blow you smote,
You seize the creature by the throat,
And drive your weapon through its brain
It wriggles into life again,
And stands erect and firm once more,
And darts its venom as before.

An error once familiar grown
Becomes our darling—and our own:
We hug it, kiss it, keep it press'd
Snugly and warmly to our breast,

And call the monster kind and good,
And would not slay it if we could.
Hydra, the snake of ancient time,
Born, bred and nurtured in the slime,
Nine-headed, under truthful skies,
Was but the type of all the lies
That in our era, as of old,
Defy assaults, however bold,
That flourish in prodigious growth
In the morass of mental sloth,
And twist and turn and press and crawl,
And leave their traces over all !

AN APPEAL TO THE PREACHERS OF ALL THE CREEDS.

I.

Cease your drowsy disputations,
  Ye who'd preach the Word divine;
Pouring out your turbid waters,
  When we thirst for living wine;
Speak the truth as if you meant it,
  And would turn the wrong to right,—
Not as if you half denied it,
  And mistook the dark for light!

II.

Like a slow and oozy river,
  Neither clear nor broad nor deep,
Flows your weary stream of doctrine,
  With a drone that lulls to sleep;
Words like yours bring no conviction,
  Prick no conscience, touch no heart,
And from sin's destructive courses
  Warn no sinner to depart.

III.

Leave your dry, unfruitful dogmas,
   Faith unreasoning, credence blind,
All the little narrow circles
   Where you wander, self-confined,
Plashing in the mire and puddle
   Of your small, sectarian pond,
Heedless of the mighty ocean
   And the boundless heaven beyond.

IV.

Is there nothing more to preach of
   Than the letter of the law,—
Nothing left to feed the people
   But the barren husk and straw,
Nothing for the unbelievers
   In a creed their souls disclaim,
But eternity of torment
   And the unconsuming flame ?

V.

Nobler themes than these invite you,
   If you'd throb as throbs the time,
And would speak to hearts responsive
   Words more human, more sublime.

"God is Love, and Love eternal;—
    All things change, but nothing dies;"
Find *this* gospel, and expound it,
    In the Bible of the skies.

VI.

O'er the starry vault of midnight
    See the countless worlds outspread,—
Homes, perchance, of nobler creatures
    Than our planet ever bred,—
Larger than the earth and fairer,
    And then limit, if you can,
God's great love to one poor corner,
    And one little creature—man.

VII.

God—our God—whose works surround us,
    Preaches in the summer wind,
In the tempest of the ocean,
    In the silence of the mind,
In the sparkle of the planets,
    In the splendour of·the sun,
In the voice of all creation,—
    "God is Love, and God is one;"

VIII.

Preaches ever, and for ever,
    That for Him who made us all
There is neither past nor future,
    Time nor space, nor great nor small,
But one vast eternal Present,
    Filled with Love for all that are,
From the dwellers in a dewdrop
    To the peoples of a star.

IX.

"Love and infinite progression,"
    These the secrets of the sky,
Open to the humblest spirit
    That but asks and wonders why;
Shut alone from hostile churches,
    Struggling each to rule, or be,
Who distress both faith and reason,—
    Blind because they will not see.

X.

Give, oh give us true religion,
    Ye who'd preach the Word divine,
We reject your tepid water,
    We're athirst for living wine.

Rouse the heart, awake the conscience,
  Look beneath you, look above;
Evil is but disobedience,—
  God is Justice—God is Love!

THE TRUE SOURCE OF BEAUTY.

The eagle on the misty mountain-top,
That overlooks whole countries stretched below
In varied beauty, has no eyes to see
The splendour of the landscape; the sea-mew,
Careering o'er the wilderness of waves,
With sunlight streaming on its snowy wings,
Knows nothing of the grandeur of the storm
That grasps the wanton billows by the crest
And twists them into cataracts of foam.
The hungry dog, made happy by a bone,
Beholds no beauty in the waving woods,
Or in the roseate glories of the dawn;
The gallant steed, whose hoof disdains the ground,
Snorts passionate joy as he surveys his mate
With supple limbs and friendly arching neck,
But fails to understand what men can see
In human beauty, be it as superb
As Aphrodite's in her youthful grace,
In perfect symmetry, divinely nude.

Mind is the mother of all loveliness,
The soul of nature, else inanimate,
That robes creation in the glorious light
That common eyes are powerless to behold,
And tunes the voiceless harmonies of heaven
To audible raptures heard but of the soul.

Mind is the Man; and he who wilfully
Neglects the priceless treasure, or in sloth
And coarse indulgence common to the brutes,
Sinks to their level, throws away the crown
That marks him king, and abdicates the right
Of high dominion given him by his God.

DAY-DREAMS.

Dozing in the sunshine
  'Mid the summer grass,
O'er my eyes half-opened
  Gorgeous visions pass :
Through my teeming fancy,
  Vagabond and free,
Stream in endless lustre
  Worlds of gramarye,—
In a long procession
  Float majestic halls,
Cities bright as amber
  Girt with golden walls,
Realms of magic splendour,
  Mine to have and hold,
And enjoy undoubting
  Till the tale is told ;
Sirens, houris, angels
  Beautiful and kind,

Flit and fly and hover
 Through my careless mind;
Kaiser! is thine empire
 Half as rich as mine?
King! canst thou surpass me
 With thy glare and shine?
Crœsus! hast thou riches
 That with mine can vie?
Pope! hast thou dominion
 Absolute as I?

AN APPEAL.

Death, when thou comest, do not linger long;
Take me home gently: I am weak—thou'rt strong!
I fear thee not, but would not have thee wait
At my bedside, or hover at my gate:
Be merciful, as all the strong should be,
And spare my struggles as my soul goes free!

ONCE ON A TIME.

Once on a time—'twas in the " Long Ago,"
When our hearts were pure as the drifted snow—
    The skies were bluer,
    The truth was truer,
The sun and the moon shed brighter rays
Than they ever shed in our later days!
Oh the time, the bonnie Gone-by !
Will its like never shine in the beautiful sky
In the sunset of life as it did in the morn ?
Oh, never again ! if the heart forlorn
Heeds not the joy that the passing hours
Offer as gifts from the heavenly powers,
And scorns to pluck the fruit from the bough
Of the ever kind and bountiful Now !
Let us enjoy the passing day
That all too rapidly fades. away,
And swell no more with sighs and frets
And unavailing though fond regrets

For the Past that was Present and offered us joy
That we did our utmost to destroy.
   'Tis the heart grown hard, 'tis the sight grown
      dull,
That draws a veil over the beautiful:
The Present has claims upon heart and head;
To-day is vigorous—Yesterday's dead!

A THOUGHT:

In the Spring Sunshine.

The flowers look up to the Sun, their God,
   And worship him with their beauty—
'Tis all their frailty has to give,
   But enough for Love and Duty.
The unfolding leaves on the forest trees
   With hope and gladness quiver,
And the birds sing praises on the bough
   To the bountiful Life-Giver.

But men delight to trade in War;
   And if they slay their brother,
They urge that Law demands the deed—
   'Tis fair as any other,;
They take no heed of the God in heaven,
   Or His sun that shines in gladness:
Pity them, birds! Pity them, flowers!
   Pity their hate and madness!

FRIENDLY DISAPPOINTMENT.

I.

STERN Disappointment! you're my friend,
  Although you're hard to bear!
I've looked for joy, and in its stead
  You've brought me near despair;
I sought for pearls of priceless worth,
  And from your cruel store
You've given me mosses from the rocks
  And pebbles from the shore.

II.

But heavy as your touch has been,
  I've learned to bear its weight,
And drawing good from seeming ill,
  I've struggled with my fate;
And when the agony has passed,
  Beheld with glad surprise
That pain and sorrow and distress
  Were blessings in disguise.

III.

I've learned that granite from the rock
    And pebbles from the tide
May be employed to useful ends
    When pearls have been denied;
So, Disappointment, do your worst!
    And, scorning to complain,
I'll stand unconquered, and confess
    You've not been sent in vain!

THE TRUE CHRISTIAN.

I.

If thou'rt a Christian
  In deed and thought,
Loving thy neighbour
  As Jesus taught,—
Living all days
  In the sight of Heaven,
And not *one* only
  Out of seven,—
Sharing thy wealth
  With the suffering poor,
Helping all sorrow
  That Hope can cure,—
Making religion
  A truth in the heart,
And not a cloak
  To be worn in the mart,
Or in high cathedrals
  And chapels and fanes,

Where priests are traders
And count the gains,—
All God's angels will say, "Well done!"
Whenever thy mortal race is run.
White and forgiven,
Thou'lt enter heaven,
And pass, unchallenged, the golden gate,
Where welcoming spirits watch and wait
To hail thy coming with sweet accord
To the holy city of God the Lord!

II.

If Peace is thy prompter,
And Love is thy guide,
And white-robed Charity
Walks by thy side,—
If thou tellest the truth
Without oath to bind,
Doing thy duty
To all mankind,—
Raising the lowly,
Cheering the sad,
Finding some goodness
Even in the bad,

And owning with sadness,
   If badness there be,
There might have been badness
   In thine and in thee,
If Conscience the warder
   That keeps thee whole
Had uttered no voice
   To thy slumbering soul,—
All God's angels will say, " Well done! "
Whenever thy mortal race is run.
   White and forgiven,
   Thou'lt enter heaven,
And pass, unchallenged, the golden gate,
Where welcoming spirits watch and wait
To hail thy coming with sweet accord
To the holy city of God the Lord !

III.

If thou art humble,
   And wilt not scorn,
However wretched,
   A brother forlorn,—
If thy purse is open
   To misery's call,

And the God thou lovest
Is God of all,
Whatever their colour,
Clime or creed,
Blood of thy blood,
In their sorest need,—
If every cause
That is good and true,
And needs assistance
To dare and do,
Thou helpest on
Through good and ill,
With trust in Heaven,
And God's good will,—
All God's angels will say, "Well done!"
Whenever thy mortal race is run.
White and forgiven,
Thou'lt enter heaven,
And pass, unchallenged, the golden gate,
Where welcoming spirits watch and wait
To hail thy coming with sweet accord
To the holy city of God the Lord!

WE DARE NOT.

We dare not, no ! we dare not do them justice,
  The great good men that flourish in our time,
The noble souls that urge mankind to effort
  By high example or by thoughts sublime ;
The praise we give them, though our hearts may feel it,
  Must find no utterance on the willing tongue,
Lest the base crowd should scorn or misinterpret
  The unselfish homage too profusely flung,
Lest they should deem it born of sordid motive,
  Or think 'tis fate whatever may befall,
That in life's cruel and incessant struggle
  Praise of the Great is injury to the Small.

Wait till they're dead ! The time to do them justice
  Is when the daisies grow upon the grave,
And rueful Memory sheds a trail of glory
  Upon the pathways of the good and brave !

The future is the heritage of greatness,
    Whether it bloom in action or in song ;
Injustice and neglect may shroud the living,
    But Death impartial rectifies the wrong !

PART II.

THISTLEDOWN AND HIGHLAND HEATHER.

TO MY OLD HIGHLAND PLAID.

I.

For forty years thou'st been mine own,
   Cozie aye and ready,
Over my breast and shoulders thrown,
   My faithful plaidie !
My sheltering shield in wintry days
   And in the nights of summer,
My pillow when the needful sleep
   Was an uncertain comer.

II.

Never hast thou been false to me,
   Cozie aye and ready,
Warm at my neck, snug at my knee,
   My faithful plaidie !
We've clomb the hills, we've tracked the streams,
   We've trod the moorland heather,
We've wandered through remotest lands,
   And braved the storms together.

III.

Since first I donned thee, fresh and new,
    Cozie aye and ready,
We have been comrades tried and true,
    My faithful plaidie !
While suits, full twenty, that I've worn,
    And spent a pile of cash on,
Have faded into shabbiness,
    And perished out of fashion.

IV.

What changes we have seen since then,
    Lingering and unready,
In fate, in circumstance, in men,
    My faithful plaidie !
Old friends, old loves, estranged and dead,
    Have dimmed to shadows only,
And flit before my mournful thought
    To whisper that I'm lonely.

V.

And when thy folds I round me wrap,
    Cozie aye and ready,
I often think it sore mishap,
    My faithful plaidie !

That thy stout fabric should endure
    When youth's fond hopes have perished,
Or the grave holds the senseless clay
    Of those I loved and cherished.

VI.

The years have robbed my limbs of strength,
    To spoil me ever ready;
But thou art staunch in width and length,
    My faithful plaidie!
Thy web is firm in warp and woof;
    But flesh and bones grown weary,
Make life no longer what it was
    When we were young, my dearie!

VII.

Stay with me still, mine ancient friend!
    Cozie aye and ready,
Until the fast approaching end,
    My faithful plaidie!
And when the hand of Fate shall snap
    The mortal chain that bound me,
I'll ask no better burial-cloth
    Than thou to wrap around me!

STRATHNAVER NO MORE.

I.

Bonnie Strathnaver,* extinct are the fires
That glowed on the hearths of our true-hearted
    sires,
Where we sat at the gloaming and learned at the
    knee
The deeds of the Clan in the days of the free.

II.

Red-handed Oppression, that calls itself Law,
Has swept through the land, spreading havoc and
    awe ;

---

* " Sutherlandshire was formerly a populous county, inhabited by a quiet, orderly, brave, religious race of men, remarkable for their fine forms, great bodily strength and high military qualities. . . . Since sheep have found their way to these pastures, this country is one wide and waste solitude. . . . Where three or four shepherds, with their dogs, can take charge of a district twenty miles in extent, it is not surprising if we wander for days without seeing the traces of human life—solitary as the sands of Africa or the immeasurable ocean."—Critical examination of Dr. MacCulloch's work on the " Highlands and Western Isles of Scotland " (Edinburgh, 1825).

And, fierce as a whirlwind, laid low in the dust
The sheltering homes of the brave and the just;

III.

Laid low to the earth the abodes of the men
That once were the glory and pride of the glen,
Who fought for their country when Duty appeal'd
And Victory summoned her sons to the field.

IV.

Brave men and true women were fruits of the line,
And grew on our moors in the old happy time,
Ere the land was considered God's gift to the few
With absolute right to possess and subdue;

V.

Ere hucksters succeeded the noble and brave,
And robbed us alike of a home and a grave,
And cared not for harvests of barley and corn,
While deer could be hunted and sheep could be
    shorn;

VI.

While cattle and grouse could be turned into gold,
And men like our fathers, those heroes of old,
Brave in heart, strong in hand, clear of purpose
    and head,
Were worthless as merchandise, living or dead.

VII.

So the cot was pulled down, and laid waste the
    kail-yard,
And turned into wilderness fruitless and hard
For the sheep or the deer and the shy ptarmigan—
For anything, everything, rather than man.

VIII.

Bonnie Strathnaver! we see thee in dreams,
Thy craigs and thy corries, thy braes and thy
    streams ;
We tread the green heath, we clamber the Bens,
And wail for the woe of the desolate glens,

IX.

And think of the time when a perishing realm,
That rivals invade and that foes overwhelm,
Shall call, but in vain, for the aid unsuborned
Of the men it misgoverned, insulted, and scorned :

X.

Shall call, but in vain, in its right of endeavour,
For the help it has banished for ever and ever
Of the clansmen, the noble, the strong and the
    brave,
Who wander afar o'er the wild western wave.

XI.

Strathnaver ! Strathnaver ! farewell evermore,
We're banished afar from thy beautiful shore ;
But cherish the hope through all sorrow and pain
That Right shall be Might in Strathnaver again !

DONALD MACLEOD.

DONALD MACLEOD! Wouldst hear his story told?
No stormy legend of the days of old—
Of war and tournament and high emprize,
Or knightly feuds beneath fair ladies' eyes;
But a true story of our modern time,
Such as befel, in cold Canadian clime,
A dozen winters past, Donald Macleod,
A poor man, one of millions, in the crowd.

A stalwart wight he was, whom but to see
Were to wish friend rather than enemy;
A smith by trade, a bluff, hard-working man,
Proud of his sires, his race, his name, his Clan.
His strong right arm could hurl a foeman down
Like ball a skittle; his broad brow was brown
With honest toil, and in his clear blue eye
Lurked strength to conquer fortune or defy.
Few were his words, and those but rough at best,
But truthful ever as his own true breast;

Of homely nature, not of winning ways,
Or given to tears, or overmuch of praise ;
But with a heart as guileless as a child's
Of seven years old that frolicks in the wilds.
Ere Donald left his shieling in the glen,
By the burnside that tumbles down the Ben
On grey Lochaber's melancholy shore,
And sighed, like others, "I return no more,"
To try his fortune in the fight of life
In a new world, with fairer field for strife
Than Scotland offers, overfilled with brains,
Yet scant of acres to reward their pains,
He woo'd with simple speech a Highland maid,
Sweet as the opening flow'ret in the shade,
And asked her, " Would she quit her native land,
Her mother's love,. her father's guiding hand,
And make another sunshine far away,
For him alone ?" She blessed the happy day
That a good man, so honest and so brave,
Had sought the heart and hand she freely gave.

To see the pair—the man so massive, strong ;
The maid so frail, yet winsome as a song—
You might have thought the oak had chosen for bride
The gowan glinting on the green hillside.

And Jeanie Cameron, happy wife was she,
Sailing with Donald o'er the summer sea,
And dreaming, as the good ship cleft the foam,
Of independence and a happy home
On that abundant and rejoicing soil
That asks but hands to recompense their toil.
And Fortune favoured them, as Fortune will
All who add strength and virtue to good-will.
And Donald's hands found always work to do,
Work well repaid, which, growing, ever grew;
Work and its fair reward, but seldom known
In the old land whence hopeful he had flown;
Work all-sufficient for the passing day,
With something left to hoard and put away.
Content and Donald never dwelt apart,
And Love and Jeanie nestled at his heart.

In summer eves, his face towards the sun,
He loved to sit, his long day's labour done,
And smoke his pipe beneath the sycamore
That cast cool shadows at his cottage door,
And hear his bonnie Jean, like morning lark,
Or nightingale preluding to the dark,
Sing the old Gaelic melancholy songs
Of Scotland's glory, Scotland's rights and wrongs,

Or true love ditties of the olden time,
Breathing of highland glens and moorland thyme.

Thus years wore on. Their sky seemed sunny blue,
Without a cloud to shade the distant view
Of happiness to come. A child was born ;
Fresh to the father's heart as light of morn,
Sweet to the mother's as a dream of heaven,—
A blessing asked, but scarcely hoped when given.
Most dearly prized ! Alas ! for human joy,
That Fortune never builds but to destroy :
The child was purchased by the mother's health ;
And Donald's heart grew heavy as by stealth
He gazed, and saw the sadness in her smile
That lit, yet half extinguished it the while ;
For, ah ! poor Jeanie was too fair and frail
To bear unscathed Canadia's wintry gale ;
And hectic roses flourished on her cheek,
Filling his heart with grief too great to speak.

Long, long, he watched her, and essayed to find
Comfort and hope. At last upon his mind
Burst suddenly the thought that he'd forego
All that he earned in that New World of woe,
And bear her back, ere utterly forlorn,
To the moist mountain clime where she was born ;

To dear Lochaber and the Highland hills,
And wave-invaded glens and wimpling rills,
Where first he found her! Late, alas! too late!

"Donald," she said, "I feel approaching fate,
And may not travel o'er the stormy sea
To die on shipboard, and be torn from thee;
Here let me linger till I go to rest;
Time may be short or long, God knoweth best.
But, as the tree that's planted in the ground,
And sheds its blossoms and its leaves around,
Dies where it lives, so let me live and die
Where thou hast brought me 'twixt the earth and
    sky.
I'd not be buried in th' Atlantic wave,
But in brown earth, with daisies on my grave;
Fresh blooming gowans from Lochaber's braes,
With Scottish earth enough, the mound to raise
Above my head. Donald, let this be done,
When your poor Jeanie's mortal race is run!"

The strong man wept. "Jeanie," was all he said,
"Oh, Jeanie, Jeanie!" and he bowed his head,
And hid his face behind his honest hands,
The saddest man in all those happy lands.

"Jeanie," he said, "ye maunna, maunna dee,
And leave the world to misery and me!"

"Donald," she answered, "woeful is the strife
That my warm heart is fighting for its life;
And much as I desire for thy dear sake,
And the wee bairn's, to live till age o'ertake,
I feel it cannot be. God's will is all;
Let us accept it, whatsoe'er befall."

And Jeanie died. She had not lain i' the mools
Three days ere Donald laid aside his tools,
And closed his forge, and took his passage home
To Glasgow, for Lochaber o'er the foam;
Alone with sorrow and alone with Love,
The two but one to lead his heart above.
And long ere forty days had run their round
Donald was back upon Canadian ground;
Donald, the tender heart, the rough, the brave,
With earth and gowans for his true love's grave.

WHEN THE CLANS ENJOY THEIR OWN AGAIN.

(Air: "*Prince Charlie's Welcome to Skye.*")

I.

THERE is plenty in the land,
If its lords would understand
Their duty to the people in the glens where they
    were born:
There is barley for the " bree,"
There are herring in the sea,
There are peats upon the moor, there is grass for
    hoof and horn,
There are kail-yards for the kail,
There is milk to fill the pail,
And farms and crofts and pastures in the shadows
    of the Ben.
And as true as dark grows light,
When the morning follows night,
The Clans shall enjoy their own again !

II.

In the happy days of old,
Ere the cruel greed of gold
Drove justice from the hearts of traders in the
soil,
There was earth to dig and plough,
There was forage for the cow,
And meal and malt and raiment for the sons of
honest toil ;
And it's coming yet ere long,
When the right shall " ding " the wrong,
And our rulers learn that cattle are of less account
than men ;
And the struggle shall be won,
And justice shall be done,
And the Clans *shall* enjoy their own again !

THE BURIAL MARCH OF KING DUNCAN.

[Tradition records that the body of King Duncan, slain by Macbeth, was carried in a solemn procession of bards and warriors from Inverness to Iona, the ancient burial-place of the kings of Scotland. Shakespeare mentions the fact in his matchless tragedy of *Macbeth*—Act II., Scene 3 when Macduff, in answer to the question, "Where is Duncan's body?" replies:

> "Carried to Colme'Kill,
> The sacred storehouse of his ancestors
> And guardian of their bones."

The name of Colme Kill, or Icolmkill, has long been superseded by that of Iona, a contraction of Innis-Shona, pronounced Innis-ona, or the "Holy Island." The chapel adjoining the cathedral is dedicated to St. Oran. The two recurring lines, in quaint old spelling, of the following ballad are taken from a funeral dirge, or coronach, of the thirteenth century, which has been reprinted in collections of legends and poetry.]

I.

Wise in council, strong in fight,
> *Every daye and aule-a,*
Foe of wrong and friend of right,
> *Christe receive. his saule-a !*
Vengeance slumbers on our path,
> And awaits the morrow,

When 'twill waken in its wrath,
  After toil and sorrow.
March we now o'er hill and glen
  On to Innis-Shona,
The place of rest he loved the best,
  The Isle of Saints—Iona !

II.

Warriors bear him to the grave
  Every daye and aule-a ;
Merciful and mild and brave,
  Christe receive his saule-a !
Bards rehearse his deeds of fame
  In our Highland story ;
All the people shout his name,
  Thinking of his glory,
Bear him over strath and hill,
  Safe to Innis-Shona,
The place of rest he loved the best,
  The Isle of Saints—Iona !

III.

Sound the pibroch as we go,
  Every daye and aule-a !
Loud and sad in wailing woe,
  Christe receive his saule-a !

Hard oppression's cruel chain
  Snapped or shrunk before him ;
Sorrow never sighed in vain
  When it would implore him.
Bear him to his honoured grave,
  Deep in Innis-Shona,
The place of rest he loved the best,
  The Isle of Saints—Iona !

IV.

St. Columba gone before,
  Every daye and aule-a !
Waits his body on the shore,
  Christe receive his saule-a !
Waits amid th' expectant ghosts
  Of the great departed,
Bards and kings and warrior hosts
  And sages noble-hearted !
Bear him proudly to the grave,
  On to Innis-Shona,
The place of rest he loved the best,
  The holy Isle—Iona.

V.

Oran's ancient shrine shall hear,
  Every daye and aule-a !

Holy anthems ringing clear,
   Christe receive his saule-a!
As we lay him in the tomb,
   The appointed portal,
Through a vestibule of gloom,
   To the home immortal.
Bear him slowly to the grave,
   Deep in Innis-Shona,
The place of rest he loved the best,
   The holy Isle—Iona.

VI.

Fire is quenched, and light is fled,
   Every daye and aule-a!
Albyn mourns her hero dead,
   Christe receive his saule-a!
If in darker days to be,
   Evil fate betide us,
Chiefs and kings as brave as he
   God will send to guide us.
Lay him in his honoured grave,
   Deep in Innis-Shona,
The holy place by God's good grace,
   The Isle of Saints—Iona!

THE CANADIAN HIGHLANDER.

I.

Thanks to my sires, I'm Highland born,
  And trod the moorland and the heather
Since childhood and this soul of mine
  First came into the world together;
I've "paddled" barefoot in the burn,
  Roamed on the braes to pu' the gowan,
Or clomb the granite cliffs to pluck
  The scarlet berries of the rowan.

II.

And when the winds blew loud and shrill
  I've scaled the heavenward summits hoary
Of grey Ben Nevis or his peers
  In all their solitary glory,
And with enraptured eyes of youth
  Have seen half Scotland spread before me,
And proudly thought, with flashing eyes,
  How noble was the land that bore me.

III.

Alas! the land denied me bread,
    Land·of my sires in bygone ages,
Land of the Wallace and the Bruce,
    And countless heroes, bards and sages;
It had no place for me and mine,
    No elbow-room to stand alive in,
Nor rood of kindly mother earth
    For honest industry to thrive in.

IV.

'Twas parcell'd out in wide domains
    By cruel law's resistless fiat,
So that the sacred herds of deer
    Might roam the wilderness in quiet,
Untroubled by the foot of man,
    On mountain-side or sheltering corrie,
Lest sport should fail, and selfish wealth
    Be disappointed of its quarry.

V.

The laws of acres deemed the clans
    Were aliens at the best, or foemen,
And that the grouse, the sheep, the beeves,
    Were worthier animals than yeomen;

And held that men might live or die
　Where'er their fate or fancy led them,
Except among the highland hills,
　Where noble mothers bore and bred them.

VI.

In agony of silent tears,
　The partner of my soul beside me,
I crossed the seas to find the home
　That Scotland cruelly denied me;
And found it on Canadian soil,
　Where man is man in life's brave battle,
And not, as in my native glens,
　Of less importance than the cattle.

VII.

And here, with steadfast faith in God,
　Strong with the strength I gained in sorrow,
I've looked the future in the face,
　Nor feared the hardships of the morrow,—
Assured that if I strove aright
　Good end would follow good beginning,
And that the bread, if not the gold,
　Would never fail me in the winning.

VIII.

And every day, as years roll on
  And touch my brow with age's finger,
I learn to cherish more and more
  The land where love delights to linger.
In thoughts by day, and dreams by night,
  Fond memory recalls, and blesses
Its heathery braes, its mountain peaks,
  Its straths and glens and wildernesses.

IX.

And hope revives at memory's call
  That Scotland, crushed and landlord-ridden,
May yet find room for all her sons,
  Nor treat .the humblest as unbidden ;
Room for the brave, the staunch, the true,
  As in the days of olden story,
When men out-valued grouse and deer,
  And lived their lives—their country's glory !

AN APPEAL TO THE CHURCHES NORTH OF THE TWEED.

I.

Gree! bairnies, gree!
Thou guid auld kirk, thou braw new tree!
And independent stark U. P.,
Tell us the good o' a' the pother,
If ane's the very same as t'other,
And each the image of his brother,—
Gree! bairnies, gree!

II.

Gree! bairnies, gree!
If ane be weak, there's strength in three,
Ye're a' but twigs o' ane good tree;
Ye waste your wit in hostile clatter,
About precedence at the platter,
So sit down cannie and grow fatter!
Gree! bairnies, gree!

III.

Gree ! bairnies, gree !
The people's hand is large and free,
And widely opened it will be,
Wi' largess well deserved and ample,
If on your foolish pride you'd trample,
And set the world a bright example,
Gree ! bairnies, gree !

IV.

Gree ! bairnies, gree !
The fiert a difference I can see,
Except in matter o' the fee :
Ye should walk cheerily togither,
And cease to fight wi' ane anither—
Nor hand aloof frae friend and brither,
Gree ! bairnies, gree !

CORN RIGS AND BARLEY RIGS.

I.

It fell upon a Lammas night,
    When corn rigs were bonnie,
Beneath the moor's unclouded light
    I held awa' to Annie;
A lang, lang promised tryste we kept,
    And 'twixt the late and early,
I took my staff into my hand,
    To meet her 'mang the barley.
Corn rigs and barley rigs,
    And corn rigs are bonnie;
I'll ne'er forget that happy night
    Amang the rigs wi' Annie.

II.

The sky was blue, the winds were still,
    The moon was shining clearly,
I proffered her baith heart and hand
    Among the rigs o' barley;

I vowed my heart was a' her ain,
  I swore to love her dearly,
And bade her name the happy day,
  Amang the rigs o' barley.
Corn rigs and barley rigs,
  And corn rigs are bonnie;
I'll ne'er forget that happy night
  Amang the rigs wi' Annie.

III.

She named the day, the first o' May,
  Her heart was beating rarely,
My blessings on her bonnie face
  Amang the rigs o' barley!
And since that time, in storm and shine,
  'Tis twenty summers fairly,
We've never rued our wooin' time
  Among the rigs o' barley.
Corn rigs and barley rigs,
  And corn rigs are bonnie;
I'll ne'er forget that happy night
  Amang the rigs wi' Annie!

THE BONNIE LASS TOCHERLESS.

I HAE my tocher in my face,
  And tocher in my voice,
And a dozen tochers in my heart,
  To bid the lads rejoice.
Tochers in honours and in lands
  May gang the gait they came,
But tochers in a lassie's love
  Are aye the bonnie same!

I hae nae tochers in the bank,
  Except the bank of truth,
And faithful love and trust in Heaven,
  And health and hope and youth.
So take me, laddie, if you will,
  And if our love endure,
We'll walk the wide world hand in hand,
  And never know we're poor!

DEFIANCE.

I.

Should evil fortune grip us fast,
  And aft it strives to fa' that,
We'll no be scared or trodden down,
  But stand erect for a' that!
We'll meet it fair, an' straight and square,
  And if it's wrang we'll right it,
And hae the pride, whate'er betide,
  To grapple wi't and fight it!

II.

The greatest griefs, if bravely met,
  Grow mean and sma' and a' that,
And if we're strong, they'll yield ere long,
  And rin awa', and a' that!
And if a nut defy our jaws,
  And we are fain to crack it,
We'll tak' a hammer in our fist,
  And spite of fate, we'll brak' it!

MY BONNIE MARY; OR, THE EMIGRANT.

I.

COME away, come away, my bonnie Mary,
Come away, come away, over the sea,
Albyn's no place for us, my bonnie Mary,
Landless and homeless wherever we be.

    But there's a land, my dear,
    Noble and grand, my dear,
    With work for the willing,
    And farms for the tilling,

Far away over the bonnie blue sea ;
Come away, come away, my bonnie Mary,
Come to the land of the brave and the free !

II.

Come away, come away, my bonnie Mary,
Come away, come away, over the tide;
Far, far behind us, my bonnie Mary,
Leaving the land where our forefathers died,

Far, far behind, my dear ;
Fortune's unkind, my dear,
Hardship's unfailing,
Grief's unavailing,
But joy is before us, and hope long denied ;
Come away, come away, my bonnie Mary,
Love is our comfort, God be our Guide !

HE'S OWER THE HILLS.

He's ower the hills that I lo'e weel,
He's ower the hills that's true and leal,
He's ower the hills and ower the sea,
An' he'll come back to marry me.

That I had gear an' he had nane
Was cause o' mickle grief and pain;
For this they parted him and me,
But no' for ever—bide a wee !

For a' my gear, wer't ten times told,
In lands, in houses, and in gold,
I'd gi'e it for one word alone,
The word that made him a' mine own.

The burnie wimplin' o'er the lea
Maun find the river and the sea,
And hearts that love, if strong as Fate,
Maun come thegither soon or late.

He's ower the hills that I lo'e weel,
He's ower the hills that's brave and leal,
He's ower the hills and ower the sea,
And he'll come back to marry me.

THE BARLEY MILLER.

My friens a' pass me coldly by
  An' glower an' glaik aboon me,
An' a' my bills come tumblin' in
  Like billows that would droon me.
    I'm low doun, doun, doun,
      Down for lack 'o' siller;
    I'm low doun, doun, doun,
      Quoth the barley miller.

The lassie that I lo'ed fu' weel,
  And courted late and early,
Has ta'en the gee (but bide a wee),
  I'm sure she'll jilt me fairly.
    I'm low doun, doun, doun,
      Down for lack o' siller;
    I'm low doun, doun, doun,
      Quoth the barley miller.

The boon companions ance I knew,
  When they and I were couthie,

Have no' a plack in a' their pack
　To lend me when I'm drouthie.
　　For I'm low doun, doun, doun,
　　Down for lack o' siller;
　　I'm low doun, doun, doun,
　　Quoth the barley miller.

And some there be who praised my wit
　When I had fouth o' siller,
Who ca' me now a doited loon
And blethrin barley miller!
　　For I'm low doun, doun, doun,
　　Doun for lack o' siller;
　　I'm low doun, doun, doun,
　　Quoth the barley miller.

An' yet I think I'll bide my time,
　Tho' Fortune sairly skelp me,
And trust brave heart and good right hand
　To comfort me and help me.
　　Although I'm doun, doun, doun,
　　Doun for lack o' siller,
　　I'll no' be doun for evermore!
　　Quoth the barley miller.

MY HEART'S IN THE HIGHLANDS.

I.

My heart's in the Highlands, my heart's in the glens,
Tracing the burnies and climbing the Bens,
Treading the heather and bracken so green,
With gowans and bluebells up-glinting between.

II.

My heart's in the land of the leal and the true,
The land of the kilt and the bonnets of blue,
Where the plaid never covered the breast of a slave,
And the lassies are fair and the laddies are brave.

III.

My heart's in the Highlands, the long summer day
Breathing the health-giving breeze on the brae,
And braving the tempests that gather below;
My heart's in the Highlands, wherever I go.

IV.

My heart's in the Highlands, in sunshine and cloud,
On the loch, in the corrie far frae the crowd;
By the rivers I love, in the glens where they flow,
My heart's in the Highlands, wherever I go!

LORD RONALD, AND THE TWO GREAT CHESTS.

I.

There lay two chests in the deep, deep earth
　Under the castle tower,
Buried there for a thousand years
　If they had lain an hour.

II.

The one contained a fearful plague
　To desolate the land,
And work worse woe than e'er befell
　From sword or flaming brand.

III.

The other held a precious gem
　Of more transcendant worth
Than all the gold that e'er was dug
　From the bowels of the earth.

IV.

They were as like in size and form,
   Reposing side by side,
As the twin blue eyes in the happy face
   Of a young and blooming bride.

V.

They were as like as the cherries twain
   That grow on the selfsame tree,
Or the droplets of the summer rain
   That falls into the sea.

VI.

And no man 'dared, though many wished,
   And had wished for ages long,
To open the lids of these awful chests
   And force their fastenings strong.

VII.

They longed for treasure, but feared the Death
   That was decreed the doom
Of the rash intruder who loosened the plague
   To feed the ravenous tomb.

VIII.

Lord Ronald was heir of the Castle lands,
  And more than tongue could tell
He loved a maiden of low degree—
  Sweet Ellen of Invernell.

IX.

She loved him truly in return,
  But ever his suit denied
Unless his sire, a proud old Earl,
  Looked favouring on his bride.

X.

But the father loved the rich red gold
  As much as the brave young son
Loved the bright gleam of Ellen's eyes
  And the ground she trod upon.

XI.

The Earl had chosen his son should wed
  A lady fair and young,
With a dowry that might tempt a duke,
  And from ancient lineage sprung.

XII.

But the wayward, love-enraptured boy
  Despised the gold and land,
And where he could not give his heart
  Refused to give his hand.

XIII.

" I'll tempt the Fates !" he suddenly said,
  As he roamed in the woods alone;
" And if I open the lucky chest,
  I'll make my love mine own.

XIV.

" My sire shall have the gold he loves
  If I open the golden chest,
And I will marry the girl I love—
  My beautiful, my best !

XV.

" And if it be my cruel fate
  To open the chest of Death,
I'll die for Ellen and bless her name
  With my departing breath."

XVI.

Lord Ronald dug with spade and pick
　From morn into the night,
And offered up an earnest prayer
　That Heaven would guide him right.

XVII.

He found the coffers side by side,
　And gazed with hope, yet dread,
Alike in hue, in form and size,
　As old tradition said.

XVIII.

With desperate haste he wrench'd the lid
　Of the one that offered first,
Hoping the best that might befall,
　And reckless of the worst.

XIX.

He wrenched and wrenched, and found within
　Nought but a parchment scroll,
On which was writ, in runic rhymes,
　" *God save the sinner's soul!*

XX.

" The plague's already in the land,
Fear not a greater pest ;
'Tis lust of gold that fills mankind :
Consult the other chest !

XXI.

Lord Ronald wiped his damp cold brow,
And breathed a prayer to Heaven :
" If I do wrong in seeking gold,
Be the offence forgiven !

XXII.

" I sin for sake of woman's love,
And not for love of pelf ;
And love no woman for her gold,
But only for herself."

XXIII.

He wrenched the lid, and wrenched again,
Till with a sudden spring
It flew wide open, and disclosed
A little golden ring,

XXIV.

Tied with a silken cord that lay
  On a scroll of parchment white,
On which was writ in runic rhymes,
  In characters of light,—

XXV.

" True love is better than all the gems
  That shine on a royal crown,
And richer in more true delight
  Than wealth can scatter down !

XXVI.

" Take thou the symbol ! If thou find
  A hand on which 'twill dwell,
With heart to ratify the pledge
  And truth to bind it well,

XXVII. '

" Thou wilt be rich, however poor
  Thy lot in life may be :
Gold is the dross—its gain is loss ;
  Love is felicity ! "

XXVIII.

Lord Ronald's sire forbore to chide ;
  And ere the day was gone
The low-born Ellen of Invernell
  Received his benison :

XXIX.

And on her wedding day she shone
  Like sunbeam through a cloud,
And gathered homage like a queen
  From all the wondering crowd.

XXX.

Her step was light, her smile was bright,
  And from her lustrous eyes
Love linked with goodness sparkled forth
  Like morning from the skies !

"GOOD NIGHT, AND JOY BE WI' YOU A'!"

THE night has been a joyous night,
But here no longer maun we stay,
Lest morning with her tell-tale light
Should dawn to beckon us away.
Wi' warnings fair we've banished care,
Nor listened ance to sorrow's ca',
But danced and sung baith old and young;—
"Good night, and joy be wi' you a'!"

Yet, happy as the hours hae been,
'Twould no be grateful to forget,
'Mid a' the pleasure we hae seen,
That time may bring us greater yet!
Our merry meeting next to be!
Meanwhile may ne'er a grief befa'
And ne'er a friend know friendship's end;
"Good night, and joy be wi' us a'!"

PART III.

LIFE, DEATH AND IMMORTALITY.

TIME AND ETERNITY.

Frail Body! cease to sue for breath,
  Thou canst not conquer in the strife:
Time was created but for Death,
  And all Eternity for Life!

TWO STUDIES OF DEATH.

In the Dark Shadow.

There hangs a shadow on the face of day,
Dark, chill, and faintly luminous with haze,
That robes the earth in one lugubrious pall;
It hushes cheerfulness, and chokes the voice
Of hope and comfort, latent in men's hearts;
It hath no shape defined or palpable:
But o'er the soulless body of the dead
Seems to proclaim, in mystic syllables,
The final victory of the greedy grave.

" Wear doleful black ! The spirit hath departed.
　Weep and lament in soul-subduing gloom;
And slowly, wearily, and heavy-hearted,
　Consign our brother to the sheltering tomb.
No more, no more his pleasant smile shall cheer us,
　No more his liberal hand shed largess free;
No more his welcome step, approaching near us,
　Shall tell of friendly intercourse to be;

No more his words shall bless the little children
  That sport and prattle round the cheerful hearth;
No more his honest laugh shall ring responsive,
  To fan the lambent flame of innocent mirth;
No more his voice shall utter words of gladness,
  To guide the lost and comfort the forlorn.
Music is hushed in all-pervading sadness,
  Eclipsed for ever is the light of morn;
The earth hath claimed him, and the earthworms riot
  Over his senseless clay : the spark hath fled.
Peace to his ashes ! Let him sleep in quiet
  Till the last trump shall sound to wake the dead."

In the Bright Sunshine.

Beside the bier there stands a radiant angel,
Invisible to unbelieving eyes,
But palpable to hope and faith and love.
Clad in white garments, lustrous and resplendent,
She turns her tender eyes in holy rapture
To the clear sky, and points her guiding finger
To the bright sunshine, bathing earth with glory,
And seems to chant, in tones of adoration,
That pulse-like ripple on a sea of silence
In harmonies ecstatic heard in heaven,
Her song of triumph o'er the conquered grave.

"Robe not your limbs in melancholy blackness,
  Nor weep disconsolate. Be bright of cheer;
Think of our brother in the eternal mansions,
  Where sorrow enters not, nor doubt, nor fear;
Where the undying spirit dwells with God,
  Partaker of His essence, heir sublime
Of all the secrets of the universe,
  Blurred and forgotten in the mists of time;
Where death is dead, and life, in perfect fulness,
  Climbs up the eternal stair of endless good,
That leads to better ever, evermore.
  In God's unspeakable Infinitude;
Obstruction knows him not, space doth not bind him;
  Limit hath no existence; time in vain
Rolls in its earthly circles to oppress him;
  He knows it not, he feels it not again.
He hath inherited the endless *Now,*
  In which the stars are but as grains of dust,
Sprinkled upon the illimitable shore
  Of the To be, the Is, the Was, the Must,
That fill the universe with life and love,—
  Life that is knowledge, love that is delight.
These are his heritage beyond the tomb,
  These are his glories in the Infinite!"

NOTHING MORE?

To eat, drink, sleep, and propagate and die-
  'Such is the invariable round
Of tasks that must be done beneath the sky
  By all who cumber the prolific ground.
But is life worth the penalties it lays
  Upon the helpless children of mankind,
If there be no Hereafter to their days,
  Or happy Immortality for mind?
If human fate were nothing more than this,
Death were delight, and nothingness were bliss!

THE RIVER AND THE SEA.

I.

Fair river of Life! I have sailed thee,
   Borne onward by favouring gales,
And landed betimes in the meadows,
   Or roamed through the beautiful vales.
I chose a fair bride in her splendour,
   And friends who were joyous and free,
And we sang and we danced and made merry,
   And never once thought of the sea.
But now we have come to its margin,
   We pause to reflect while we may,
Of the present, the past, and the future,
   And the night that comes after the day.

II.

Dark ocean of Death! I must cross thee,
   And travel to regions unknown,
Where I trust that my God will receive me
   In the light that encircles His throne;

To give my nude spirit expansion
  To soar, and eternally soar,
'Mid splendours of heights empyréan
  And the infinite Evermore!
Dark Ocean! there's brightness beyond thee,
  My soul can behold it afar,
And 'twill pass o'er thy cloud-covered waters
  With God for its compass and star!

LIVING AND DYING.

We only live that we may die,
If Fate this problem give ;
May not its nobler answer be,
We die that we may live ?

THE LITTLE CHINK.

I.

A CHINK upon the dungeon wall
  Lets in the light of day,
Where ministering angels float unseen
  And sparkle in the ray.
The prisoner when the night is clear
  Forgets his bolts and bars,
And gazes through the friendly rift
  At moonlight and the stars.
His soul 'mounts to them, though his flesh
  Pines in a living tomb;
And heaven's bright orbs hold high discourse
  To cheer him in the gloom.

II.

Poor prisoner! type of all condemned
  To tread life's weary round,
And feel the pressure of the chain
  That binds us to the ground.

We groan behind our prison bars,
But through a narrow chink
Have glimpses of the light of God
More glorious than we think.
The rift of Reason is but small,
But through the rift we see
The light Divine—the hope and faith
Of Immortality.

CAN THIS BE ALL?

I.

To come into the world
Without our own consent,
And live our destined years
In ceaseless discontent;
To struggle in the gloom
Behind life's dungeon wall,
And pine in vain for light,—
 Can this be all?

II.

To drag a weary chain
Over a rugged road,
And groan at each remove
And shifting of the load;
To feel the animal curse
That weighs on great and small
Of slavery to the flesh,—
 Can this be all?

III.

To pace the same dull round
On each recurring day,
For seventy years or more,
Till strength and hope decay ;
To trust and be deceived,
And standing, fear to fall
And find no resting-place,—
　　Can this be all ?

IV.

To strive to find the truth,
But fail for want of light,
To pierce the heavy gloom
That shrouds it from our sight ;
To dash our aching heads
Against the obstructing wall
That Reason cannot pass,—
　　Can this be all?

V.

To know not whence we come
Or whither we shall go
When this poor life has pass'd,
With all its weight of woe,

And doubt if life be life
When loss and grief befall,
Or whether we but dream,—
    Can this be all?

VI.

To live as lives the grass
And the autumnal grain,
Born of the sun and sod
And fertilising rain,
And pass away like them
At scythe and sickle's call,
And leave no trace behind,—
    Can this be all?

VII.

And if we propagate
By Love's supreme decree
Poor wretches like ourselves
Predoomed to misery,
To run the selfsame course
In doubt and fear and thrall
From the cradle to the tomb,—
    Can this be all?

VIII.

And if by sorrow nursed
We sit alone and weep
Beside the grass-grown mound
Where our belov'd ones sleep,
And envy them their rest
Beneath the grave's cold pall,
Our desolate hearts inquire,—
　Can this be all ?

IX.

Ah, no !　Fate has not launched
So cruel a decree,
Or whatsoe'er we are,
Twere better not to be ;—
Eternity is ours,
And man that seems so small
Shall live again in heaven
　With God his All in all !

DIVINE ANANKÊ.

GREAT mother of the teeming universe,
Supporter of the fabric of the skies,
Guider of stars and planets in their course,
Parent of men and nations, beasts and birds,
And all that crawl and creep and float and fly,
Anankê, author of all life and death,
Why should we strive to undermine thy wall,
Or climb above it in a vain attempt
To solve the awful mysteries of heaven,
Or lift the smallest corner of the veil
That shrouds from finite sense the Infinite?
Why wreck the petty skiff we call our mind
Against the impassable rocks that bar the way
We'd fairly travel to the Dark Beyond,
That after Death we may perchance behold
And find revealment of the hidden things
Of matter and of spirit, space and time,

And good and evil, portions of our self?
Let us be humble in imprisonment,
And patient in our hopeless ignorance:
God is necessity.   Necessity is God.

IN THE ELMER WOODS.

The great high-spreading elmer tree
That waves to the winds its branches free
Must fall beneath the woodman's blows
Ere the time of the winter snows.
Such is the woodman's high decree,
Fate's minister for him who owns
Land and forest, grass and stones,
And all the woodland spreading wide,
And corn and pastureland beside.

If such the doom of the lordly tree,
That stands so firm, so fair, so free,
May not the Fates reserve for me,
At woodman Death's appointed time,
A downfall in my manhood's prime?
And in the elm tree's girth and bole
May there not lurk in Time's control
The boards and planks that workmen true
Shall saw and fashion, nail and screw,

Till they construct a coffin fine
To hide this perishing flesh of mine ?

Perhaps ! But till the hour arrives
I and the tree can live our lives :
Its boughs can wave in the summer air,
And birds build nests in its branches fair ;
The rains refresh it at morns and eves,
And the moonlight slumber on its leaves ;
And I, content with the passing day,
May find enjoyment while I may,
And laugh with care-unfettered mind,
Living and loving and resigned,
And drink, instead of the dews and rain,
My " Marcobrünner" and champagne,
And interchange with men and books
Thoughts and fancies and friendly looks.
The tree knows nothing of its fate,
Nor I of mine, and so I wait
In fearless trust, whate'er befall,
That a good God reigns·over all.

THE GOOD OF IT.

WHAT is the good of being born
Into this world of hate and scorn,
Naked and feeble and forlorn?
What is the good, though childhood's years
May have their smiles as well as tears,
Though youth, which recks not of the morrow,
Partakes of joy as well as sorrow?
What is the good, though love is bright
And robes the world with rosy light
In the first dawning of its day,
If evening sees it fade away?
And when, the longer that we crawl
On earth's too miserable ball,
The more we feel that life is vain,
And that man's heritage is pain!
What is the good of lengthened life,
If purchased by perennial strife,
When sordid wants and grinding cares
Surge up for ever unawares,

And fond illusions, one by one,
Exhale, like dewdrops in the sun,—
What is the good?
                    Perchance our birth
Is but probation on the earth,
And that as soon as life begins
We have to suffer for the sins
Committed in another sphere,
All to be expiated here?
Support us, Faith—if we'd rebel!
This is the answer: Earth is hell,
Or purgatory, to refine
By pangs of punishment divine,
And fit the immortal soul to soar
Towards perfection evermore,
And flourish in celestial light,
Partakers of the Infinite!

LIFE'S LITTLE DAY.

I.

THE DAWN.

An innocent infant, with blue, earnest eyes,
Paddling upon the shore with glad surprise
At each new object that attracts its sight—
Shells on the beach, or sea-mews gleaming white,
Or the dark billows glittering far away
In the first radiance of the coming day.

II.

EARLY MORNING.

The sun is up, and bathes the eastern sky
With floods of light; the tide is rising high,
And the boy's thought, with far-extending scope
Impatient of the present, dwells with hope
On the unknown but slow-approaching time
When he shall creep no more, but mount and climb.

III.

The Forenoon.

The glowing glorious noon has not yet shed
Its radiance, but the moving mists have fled,
And the blood courses warmly through his veins,
And passion wakens with its joys and pains
And dear delights far short of his desires,
And physical energies and mental fires.

IV.

Midnoon.

Noon! and the widening landscape, full revealed,
Shows crags and pitfalls that the morn concealed,
Which he must pass in safety if he can,
Now that he's reached the dignity of man,
And sees the toils he's bound to undergo
If he would flourish in a world of woe;
The perils that beset him ,on his path,
The jealousies, the treacheries, and the wrath
That he must conquer if he'd stand erect
And win a footing in the world's respect,
Like a true soldier in the ennobling fight
Against the daily wrong that wars with right.

V.

AFTERNOON.

Wearied and worn, but hopeful still and bold,
With head still clear and heart not yet grown old,
He rests a little from the moil of life,
And takes a respite from perennial strife,
To look back cheerfully on duty done
And fruitful triumphs well and bravely won.

VI.

SUNSET.

Clad in full glory in the crimsoning west,
The sun's last radiance gilds the ocean's breast,
And the day darkens in the east afar,
While on Night's forehead gleams the evening star,
Herald of heavenly hosts as yet unseen,
That fill with splendours all the vast serene.

VII.

NIGHT.

'Tis night, and not a cloud upon the blue,
And countless glories burst upon his view
In all the dread magnificence of heaven.
He bends with awe and feels his sins forgiven,
And hears the angels' voices chanting high,
"Mount, kindred spirit, mount into the sky!"

IMMORTALITY.

" Man never dies—but all men die,"
Is this the immortality
We fondly crave? When we are gone
Are we as heedless as a stone
Of all that was or is to be?
Alas, for thee! Alas, for me!
The blooming rose, the mounting flame,
Might, could they think, repeat the same
Sad query to the passer-by,
And ask if they but live to die;
And if the life that moves them now
Is all the cruel fates allow.
Woe's me! like gudgeons in a glass,
We turn and twist, but cannot pass,—
In vain we'd work the problem out.
Our senses fail us, and we doubt;
And when to doubt is but to grieve,
Is it not better to believe?

EUTHANASIA.

The king of terrors, such as cowards feign
In the wild nightmare of the heart and brain,
Is to the wise the Lord of life and light,
And hath no terrors to their thought or sight.
No vengeful arrows bristle in his hands
To scatter sorrow o'er the peaceful lands;
But love angelic from his brooding wings
Drops on the earth and all created things;
And his calm eyes, with pure celestial sheen,
Glow through the universe with light serene.

The foolish crowd, unchristian-like, behold
In the dark grave nought but the encircling mould
That wraps the body, when the soul elate
Takes joyous wing to the celestial gate,
At which Death stands to welcome mortals in,
Freed from corruption, purified from sin.
Death is but change of vesture for the soul—
New scope, new strength, and life beyond control
Of time and space and earth's impeding clod,
With bliss eternal in the love of God!

A MOTH AND A MAN.

QUESTIONS.

MOTH, that art fluttering, flying
　　Up in the sunny air,
What dost thou know of the wonders
　　That earth and sky. declare?
Nothing! oh, nothing! nothing,
　　Except that the world is fair!

Man, that art creeping, crawling
　　Painfully on the earth,
What dost *thou* know of the riddle
　　Of life and death and birth,
Of the purpose of existence,
　　And what thy soul is worth?

THE MAN'S REPLY.

The moth and myself know nothing;
　　We're both the slaves of sense,

And only see in a circle
  Through a medium dark and dense,
And flourish for short season,
  Only to travel hence.

The insect knows no sorrows,
  And, happier far than I,
Takes life without inquiry,
  Under the clear blue sky.
I know that I am mortal—
  Born but to suffer and die!

IN PROSPECT OF DEATH.

DEAR Mother Death! on thy placid face
   I look like a loving child,
And know thou wilt purify my soul
   From all that hath defiled.
I've no regret at leaving a world
   So weary and full of woe;
Then take me, Death, whenever thou wilt,
   Thou'lt find me ready to go.

I feel the healthful breeze of life
   That flows through the open door,
Through which my spirit prepares to pass
   And to mount for evermore
Up to the highest heights of heaven,
   Freed of the bodily clod,
To learn and learn for ever and aye
   The mysteries of God.

Farewell! farewell! O dungeon clay!
   Farewell! O struggling breath!
And welcome to the gentle touch
   Of liberating Death!
Float me and waft me and carry me up,
   Defiant of time and space,
To the throne of my Father and my God
   And the radiance of His face!

INCOMPREHENSIBLE FINITUDE.

Man's senses fail to comprehend
How anything that *is* can end:
That all things change we see and know,
Life into death, joy into woe;
But something into nothingness
Transcends the reason to express:
'Tis felt and seen—not understood,
There is no law of finitude.
If this be true for worlds that roll,
Is it not true for life and soul?
For life and love in endless range,
Undying death—eternal change?

TWO MIGHTY SISTERS.

Two sisters, angels, twins in love and might,
Viceregents of the Lord of life and light,
And agents of His everlasting will,
Pérvade the universe, and fill
The stars and galaxies that roll
Through infinite space, the body of God's soul;
The one serene and pale, with pensive face,
Seems sad at heart, though sadness has no place
In her celestial mind, for love divine
Governs her thought, and with celestial shine
From her angelic and benignant eyes
Sheds heavenly pity through the awful skies.

The other, beautiful as she,
Radiant as sunlight or a peaceful sea,
Scatters perpetual morning through the stars,
And guides them God-ward in their heavenly cars,
While from her wings outspread and eyes all-seeing
She drops perpetual bliss of being;
Her looks illumine heaven and earth,
Balancing loss by gain, and death by birth.

Her earnest sister, passing o'er the lands,
Holds in the hollow of her hands
The mightiest empires, flushed with pride of power,
And in the fulness of the destined hour
Strips them of glory and of fame,
And puffs them out like the ephemeral flame
That dies for lack of fuel, and is flung
Back to the nothingness from which it sprung,
Without a record on the page of time,
Shade of a shade—faint echo of a chime
That rang a moment and was hushed for ever,
And stifled in its own endeavour
To make itself be heard above the din
Of jarring discords in a world of sin.

Her bright-eyed sister, smiling at her side,
　　Welcomes new nations to supply their place
In equal majesty to those that died,
　　To run like them their short appointed race.
Life follows Death, and Death is mother of Life—
Light comes of darkness—peace is born of strife—
And renovation tracks destruction's path
To heal the ravage of its seeming wrath,
And fill the gaps that destiny has riven
In the eternal scroll and luminous book of heaven.

Poor little mortals ! know that Death's your
    friend,
And builds again in innocence and joy
What she was powerless to destroy,
And in a chain that stretches without end
Links star to star, and sun to sun,
In everlasting unison,
And gives the children of a perishing earth
Angelic wings in new eternal birth,
To soar and soar—for ever, evermore
Up to the heaven of heavens, and starry floor—
To Love, to Know, to Worship—and Adore !

BONDAGE.

In youth my body was my joy,
A bank from which I loved to borrow;
In age it works me sore annoy,
And pays its debts in care and sorrow.
In youth I plucked the wayside rose
Of sensual pleasure, blooming o'er me;
In age the bloom no longer blows,
And thorns and brambles sprout before me.
O body! thou'rt a treacherous friend,
And lendest help but to deceive us,
Until, our bondage at an end,
Death bids the pitying grave receive us.

AN INVOCATION AND AN ASPIRATION.

I.

Come to me, Death: I fear thee not;
Thou'rt nothing but a change I wot.
If for the worst, 'tis God's behest;
If for the better, it is best.
I'm but a fancy in a dream,
I'm but a straw upon the stream,
I'm but a ripple on the sea,
An atom in Immensity.

II.

Yet no; I have diviner trust,
I am no speck, no grain of dust,
But child of God, and heir sublime
Of life beyond the reach of time—
Life unconfined by earthly bars,
And as eternal as the stars,
That live and love as well as I,
My fellow-creatures of the sky.

LITTLE GREATNESS.

WE despise the passing hour
  Because it seems so small
And so much less than the world
  On which we creep and crawl.
But is the little so little,
  On earth's very little ball?
Or is anything great or little?—
  God knows, who is All in all.

A GRAVE.

Put me in, and cover me up
  With wholesome earth,—no more I crave:
A tombstone is but waste of wealth,
  And fails to sanctify the grave.
Countless millions of men and women
  As good as I, or better maybe,
Rot in the earth without memorial:
  Why should you place one over me?
'Twould last perhaps for fifty years,
  If no one cared for the perishing stone,
Or carved no foolish lies upon it,
  To make survivors blush or groan;
Plant pale·primroses if you will,
  Or gem-like daisies 'mid the grass,
They'll lend a beauty to the ground,
  Or preach a sermon as you pass.

BODY AND SOUL.

I.

I WOULD not that my mind should die
  Before the mortal flame,
And perish into nothingness,
  Like an extinguished flame.
While body with ignoble needs,
  And slavery to the clay,
Lived on, unconscious of its loss
  And hastening to decay.

II.

Thus did I sigh, and quite forgot,
  With care-o'erclouded brow,
That ever with the immortal soul
  Dwells an eternal Now.
That all our faculties of sense,
  Though seeming great, are small,
And but the windows of the mind,
  And openings in the wall;

III.

That when the imprisoned spirit looks
  Beyond its dungeon bars,
It longs to reach its heavenly home,
  And travel through the stars,
Freed from the burden of the flesh
  That clogs its upward flight,
And darkens to its wistful gaze
  The wonders of the light.

IV.

Mute, blind, and fettered though it be,
  It is but for a time;
When rescued from its penal chain,
  And in immortal prime,
It shall enjoy the glorious Now,
  In nobler spheres than this,
With myriad senses, every one
  A doorway into bliss.

LIFE.

SEVENTY journeys round the sun,
   Cares and sorrows, great and small;
Toils and troubles, sighs and tears:
   That is all—that is all.

Love that blooms in summer hours
   And decays ere winter's fall,
Morning freshness, lost ere night:
   That is all—that is all.

Fame that whispers in our ears,
   Joy to come at merit's call,
Borne upon the breath of fools:
   That is all—that is all.

Wealth, that may be sought and won,
   If we'd climb or if we'd crawl,
And but worthless when possess'd:
   That is all—that is all.

Mound of earth, six feet by two,
   Shut from every pain and thrall,
Birth-right, death-right, both in one:
   That is all—that is all!

AMRITA.

Soar, my freed spirit, sin-forgiven,
Soar to thy long-lost home in heaven!
Soar to the light of perfect day,
A living portion of its ray.
Loosed from the impeding clogs of earth
And all the shackles of thy birth,
Thou'lt find there's work that must be done
Beyond the pathways of the sun,
And that eternity may be
Too narrow for thine energy,
If thou wouldst truly seek to know
All that the universe can show
Of love and hope and high endeavour,
Working for ever and for ever.
Rest is but death in part or whole,
And is not spoken of the soul!
   Life, life eternal, thou art mine!
Life, Love, and Knowledge, gifts divine,

That clear the way to worlds unknown,
That guard the footstool of God's throne,
Life, linked to body, frail no more,
Or slave to sorrow as before,
A prey to suffering and to need,
Ignoble in its daily thought and deed ;
But pregnant with celestial fire,
To glow, to sparkle and aspire,
To flourish in eternal bloom,
Defiant of the engulfing tomb,
With senses not confined to five
Poor outlets for the narrow hive
In which our faculties are held
By bondage of the flesh compelled,
But streaming through a thousand pores,
That open like enchanted doors,
Disclosing each a new delight,
Beyond the pleasures of the sight,
Beyond the raptures of the ears,
Pealing music of the spheres,
Till heaven itself, in sense enshrined,
Possesses all the immortal mind,
And breathes the tidings great and free
Of progress in eternity.

THE LOST ME.

I.

Whither has fled the undying Me,
  The "Me" that I knew in a bygone day;
My other self in the times of old,
  When life was in its morn of May,
Ere it had ripened to leafy June,
  With its warmer, wider, and lustier scope,
Nor lavished the wealth of its summer bloom
  For due fulfilment of my hope?

II.

"Me" and I could climb the mountains
  Up to their very topmost crest,
Or cleave the billows with vigorous sinews,
  And calm, unruffled, defiant breast.
Me and I could face the tempest,
  Braving its perils undismayed,
And revel in the pride of youth
  As courage or indifference bade.

III.

Where has he gone ? to which dim part ?
  Has he utterly vanished beyond recall,
The happy Me, that hated to doubt,
  And found belief and good in all ?
When heart and brain and body and soul,
  Flushed and stored with electric fire,
And nothing seemed too great or high
  For mad ambition to desire.

IV.

When every man was honest and brave,
  And every woman was fair and true,
And love was robed in heavenly light
  For ever beautiful and new,—
When Fancy·rode the steeds of Reason,
  Goading and spurring them, free and wild,
And every cloud had a golden border,
  And every storm a rainbow child.

V.

Alas ! another " Me " has entered
  Into my spirit and my brain,
Unlike the Me that once I cherished
  But was not destined to retain.

The wretched Me that has taken his place
Is old and sad and feeble of limb;
His good right hand has lost its cunning,
His voice is weak, his eyes are dim.

VI.

He roams no more the tangled wild-wood,
He scales no more the mountain height,
But sits in his easy chair reflecting
That after noontime comes the night;
His fond illusions are dead and buried
In the grave of the bygone years,
Dug by the spade of disappointment
Too oft in agony and tears.

VII.

"Me, oh Me! why hast thou left me?"
Strong is its faith—the soul replies:
"Thy earthly vesture fits no longer,
New garments wait thee in the skies;
Crippled by time, thou'rt bound to travel
The beaten path that all have trod—
Thou'lt find eternity before thee,
And love and light at the throne of God!"

THE DAY'S MARCH.

I.

Marching! marching! marching!
  On to the city of Death,
Nearer and ever nearer
  In every step and breath;
Bound to enter its portals,
  To rest when the day is done--
Marching with the moments
  And following as they run!

II.

Pleasant it was, and sunny,
  When I started on the way
To tread the leafy woodlands
  And the fresh green meads of May:
To hear the skylark singing
  On the fringes of the morn,
And gather wayside blossoms
  Or wreaths of the white hawthorn.

III.

To sport with the little maidens,
  Or sit beneath the tree,
When the drill of the books was over
  And the limbs and the mind were free;
To laugh and prattle and frolic,
  Or build up fairy schemes
In the palaces of Cloudland,
  And people them with dreams.

IV.

Till one as fair as daylight
  Enthralled my willing heart,
And we marched together onward
  And vowed we'd never part;
Vowed the vow and kept it,
  And felt in the pride of youth
That life was a brave possession
  When cheered by love and truth.

V.

I carolled in the morning
  To many a joyous tune,
I planned the good of my fellows
  In the flush of the sunny noon,

And held fast hold in the twilight
  To the faith of early prime,
That the good might grow to the better
  In the fulness of the time.

VI.

Marching, ever marching
  Amid confronting foes,
I trampled down obstructions
  Defiant as they rose ;
Or wounded in the conflict,
  I gathered strength anew,
And dared the hardest fortune
  To daunt me or subdue !

VII.

Pleasant it was to linger
  Under the blessèd skies,
To walk with the noble-hearted,
  The brave, the good, the wise ;
To hold high converse with them,
  And learn the truths they taught
And gather wit and wisdom
  From the interchange of thought.

VIII.

And now, as the night approaches,
  Mine eyes behold, afar,
The crimsoning gold of the sunset
  And the gleam of the evening star;
And beyond, in the shadowy distance,
  Dim seen on the misty height,
The domes of Death's dark city
  O'er-canopied with light,—

IX.

The light, the love, the glory,
  Into which my soul shall soar;
Darkness and death behind me,
  Eternity before:
Leaving my earthly vesture
  In the earthly mother sod,
To wear angelic garments
  In the mansions of my God.

THE JOYS OF SEVENTY.

I.

I'm old and ready to depart,
  I've passed the threescore years and ten,
But still keep corners in my heart
  For honest women and brave men ;
I love to see on beauty's cheek
  The bloom that pleases younger eyes,
And find enjoyment when I seek
  Among the witty and the wise.

II.

My pulses throb when coming years
  Presage the triumph of the right,
Mine eyes suffuse with wholesome tears,
  Or glow with sympathetic light,
When great unselfish deeds are done
  That rival in our sordid age
The noblest victories ever won
  Attested upon history's page.

III.

I love the modest wayside flowers,
   The dawn, the moon, the evening grey;
The pleasant sunshine and the showers,
   The gloom of night, the blaze of day;
I love the garden and the wild,
   The woodland and the barren shore,
The artless prattle of a child,
   Or memories of the days of yore.

IV.

I love a lover, prize a friend,
   And joy in every joy that's pure,
And, knowing grief must have an end,
   Make light of ills I cannot cure:
I love my fellows all I can,
   Hate Hate, scorn Scorn, and loathe a lie,
And, part of God's eternal plan,
   I'm pleased to live, content to die.

NIRVANA.

Goddess benign !
Great Mother divine,
Lay me to sleep on thy beautiful breast ;
Weary of life
And renewal of strife,
I ask but oblivion—I pray but for rest !
Sink me to nothingness ! robe me in death ;
Lull me and soothe me and stifle my breath,
Deaden mine ears to the cry of the crowd,
Its doubts and contentions,
Its feuds and dissensions,
The groans of the humble, the shouts of the proud.
What have I·done in the ages departed,
That I should remain to float hopelessly on—
A waif on the ocean, a mote in the sunshine,
A sound that is silenced, a light that has shone ?

Life hath no charms for me,
Death no alarms for me ;

Peace may be broken, and rest have an end!
Come then, Oblivion, my hope and my friend;
　　　Come and possess me,
　　　Absorb me and bless me;
　　　Beautiful nothingness,
　　　Heightless and fathomless,
Life's final glory and crown of completion,
Refuge eternal from sorrow and pain;
Love is but lust to replenish the planet
With slaves and oppressors that cumber the soil;
Fame's but a blast on a wearisome trumpet,
And wealth is but mockery, burden and toil.
Holy Nirvana! Heaven's true fulfilment!
Essence of all things! Destroyer of time!
Victor of destiny! Mother of ages!
Born unbegotten, eternal, sublime!
Grant me, oh, grant me the boon that I crave:
Dreamless beatitude—peace in the grave!

LA BELLE MORTE.

I.

Oh, Death! you are my comrade,
  My comrade and my friend;
Come, sit beside me on the bed
  Cheerily to the end.
I'm not the least afraid of you,
  And shrink not from your touch,
And feel in presence of your smile
  That you can teach me much.

II.

You are not hideous to my sight,
  Your voice is like a hymn;
Your eyes are filled with heavenly light
  Like those of seraphim.
You bear no javelin in your hand
  To pierce me to the heart,
But whisper words of peace and love
  That warn me to depart.

III.

You tell me things I never knew,
  Or cared to understand;
And show me things I never saw,
  Till guided by your hand:
The worthlessness of human life,
  That men most fondly prize,
Compared with the immortal hopes
  That blossom in the skies.

IV.

. Bright hopes that fill the expectant mind
  When we discourse together,
And I behold through wintry storms
  The heavenly summer weather.
You preach to me and prophesy,
  That when the rags I wear
Fall from my soul and leave it nude
  In sunshine and the air,

V.

I shall assume angelic robes,
  Unweighted by the clod,
And float as rapidly as thought
  Through all the realms of God.

And learn, as death unseals my eyes
  From films of earthly night,
The secrets of the Universe
  And the mysteries of the Light.

THE SOUL HOVERING OVER THE BODY TAKES JOYOUS LEAVE.

I.

Body ! that once wert a noble shrine
For a soul to dwell in, no more thou'rt mine.
Thou wert a palace in youth's bright day,
But the walls of the palace have crumbled away ;
The burdensome years and the physical chain
Of desire and pleasure—of grief and pain,
Have bought the penalty of their birth
And weighed thee down to thy mother earth ;
Thy glory's fled with the days of yore,
Farewell, frail body, for evermore !

II.

The robes thou gavest me to wear
Are torn and tattered beyond repair ;
New garments of celestial dyes
Await me in the friendly skies,
To which I joyfully return
Imperishable and eterne.

Thou held'st me by a tyrant's tether
When thou and I were linked together,
But now I'm free to fly and soar,
Farewell, frail body, for evermore !

III.

Thine eyes, that circumscribed my sight
And dulled the fulness of perfect light,
Are growing dimmer, while mine behold
The glory of the heavens unroll'd ;
Clear to my vision, extending wide,
Freed of obstruction, and purified
Of all the stain received from thee
In the prison of thy mortality ;
I'm gliding through the eternal door,—
Farewell, frail body, for evermore !

IV.

Thou hadst few secrets to disclose,
Little secrets of joys and woes,
And yearnings for the imperfect joy
That time but gave thee to destroy.

Now heaven's own secrets flood my gaze,
Of love and ecstasy and praise,
And Godlike progress and endeavour,
That lift me up for ever and ever!
I tread already the azure floor,—
Farewell, frail body, for evermore!

ON THE DEATH OF A GREAT MAN.

Bury his faults in the grave where we've laid him,
  Speak not his name but with blessings and sighs;
Hard is the heart that would seek to upbraid him,
  So great as he was and so low as he lies!

High were his aims and untarnished his honour,
  Danger he scorned in the pathways of right;
England shall miss, when the cloud is upon her,
  Him who oft led her –through darkness to light.

Weep, England, weep, for the mighty departed,
  Write his pure name on thy worthiest page;
Nobly he lived, though he died broken-hearted,
  And moulded to justice the mind of his age!

APPENDIX.

CHARLES MACKAY'S LAST POEM.

CHARLES MACKAY, the eminent poet and journalist, died in London on Christmas Eve, 1889. Up to a late hour in the evening of Sunday, December 22nd, he was engaged in reading the "Life and Works of Robert Burns," his favourite author, and during that day he seems to have whiled away the time by the composition of the following graceful stanzas, written in the Scottish manner, his love for his native country and dialect being one of his strongest characteristics. Finishing the poem, he dated it, in a somewhat tremulous handwriting, "Dec. 22, 1889," and then went quietly to the bed from which, though he knew it not, he was never again to rise. He passed away peacefully on the Tuesday morning, unconscious of suffering, his face in death assuming a singularly impressive look of wisdom and placidity,—one curious circumstance being that the right hand, which had written so much and so unweariedly, folded itself, in the last long sleep, into the customary position for holding the pen, and so remained. The last two lines of the poem here published, touchingly imply the poet's instinctive spiritual sense of his approaching release from all earthly labour.

"MY WIFE'S A WINSOME WEE THING." *

I.

My wife's a winsome wee thing,
    Wed twenty years or mair,
And aye the bonnier growing,
    As baith mine eyes declare.
'Tis love that made her bonnie,
    And love that keeps her sae,
In spite o' Time and Fortune,
    On Life's uncannie way.

II.

Love scares awa' the wrinkles
    From aff her smooth white brow,
And duty done through good and ill
    Aye keeps her conscience true,—
And yields her happy peace of mind,
    If e'er the world goes wrong,
And turns the murmur of lament
    Into a cheerful song.

* The title alone of this poem, but neither the idea nor the
treatment, is borrowed from Robert Burns.—AUTHOR'S NOTE.

III.

The kisses gather on her lips
　　Like blossoms on the rose,
And kindly thoughts reflect the light
　　That in her bosom glows,—
As wavelets in a running stream
　　Reflect the noontide ray,
And sparkle with the light of heaven
　　When rippling on their way.

IV.

She is a winsome wee thing,
　　And more than twenty year
She's twined herself about my heart
　　By all that can endear;
By all that can endear on earth,
　　Foreshadowing things above,
And lead my happy soul to heaven,
　　Rejoicing in her love!

Dec. 22nd, 1889.